CANDIDE

BY VOLTAIRE

VOLTAIRE (1694–1778). Highly respected French Enlightenment writer, famous in the eighteenth century as a philosopher, satirist, historian, letter-writer, critic, dramatist, novelist and poet.

François Marie Arouet, who later adopted the name of Voltaire, was born in 1694. He was the son of a notary and was educated at a Jesuit school in Paris. Determined on a literary career, he gained an introduction to the intellectual life of Paris and soon became known as a writer of satires and odes. However, in 1717–18 he served a six-month term of imprisonment in the Bastille, as punishment for his satire on the Regent, and between 1726 and 1729 he was exiled to England. His epic poem *La Henriade* was published in 1724, and exulted him to a place by Homer and Virgil in the eyes of his contemporaries. His *Philosophic Letters* (1733) are a harsh indictment of the French system of government, in opposition to the freer reign he discovered in England, and were shocking enough not to be allowed on sale anywhere in France. He spent the next fifteen years at the country seat of Madame de Châtelet and here he wrote his most popular tragedies and also *Zadig*, a philosophical Eastern tale, which contained many of his wittiest and cleverest ideas. After Madame de Châtelet's death, he visited the court of Frederick the Great, where he completed his important historical work *Essay on Customs* and began his *Philosophic Dictionary*, which was not published until 1764. In 1759 he published his best-known work, *Candide*, a cunning satire which pretends to espouse the theory that 'all is for the best in the best of all possible worlds', then skilfully and hilariously destroys it. He triumphantly returned to Paris, from where he had been exiled for so long, and died in 1778 at the age of eighty-four.

Candide is undoubtedly Voltaire's masterpiece. A brilliant satire of the misplaced optimism and ignorance prevalent around him, this timeless story still retains its relevance and biting wit.

PENGUIN POPULAR CLASSICS

CANDIDE

VOLTAIRE

PENGUIN BOOKS

PENGUIN BOOKS

Published by the Penguin Group
Penguin Books Ltd, 80 Strand, London WC2R ORL, England
Penguin Putnam Inc., 375 Hudson Street, New York, New York 10014, USA
Penguin Books Australia Ltd, Ringwood, Victoria, Australia
Penguin Books Canada Ltd, 10 Alcorn Avenue, Toronto, Ontario, Canada M4V 3B2
Penguin Books India (P) Ltd, 11 Community Centre, Panchsheel Park,
New Delhi – 110 017, India
Penguin Books (NZ) Ltd, Cnr Rosedale and Airborne Roads, Albany, Auckland,
New Zealand
Penguin Books (South Africa) (Pty) Ltd, 24 Sturdee Avenue, Rosebank 2196, South Africa

Penguin Books Ltd, Registered Offices: 80 Strand, London WC2R ORL, England

www.penguin.com

First published 1759
Published in Penguin Popular Classics 1997
Reprinted in the present form 2001

2

Printed in England by Cox & Wyman Ltd, Reading, Berkshire

CONTENTS

CANDIDE, or OPTIMISM

CHAPTER I

THE CASTLE OF THUNDER-TEN-TRONCKH

ONCE upon a time, in the province of Westphalia, at the castle of his lordship the Baron von Thunder-ten-Tronckh, there lived a boy of very sweet disposition. His mind could be read in his face. He was fairly intelligent, yet his general outlook was one of utter simplicity. Probably this was why he acquired the name of Candide.

The older servants of the household suspected that he was the son of his lordship's sister, the reputed father being a neighbouring landowner. The sister had refused to marry him, although he was an agreeable and worthy man, because his coat-of-arms had only seventy-one quarterings—the others having disappeared in the storms of time.

The Baron was one of the most powerful noblemen in Westphalia; as was evidenced by the fact that his castle had a great gate and windows, and its hall was hung with tapestry. The dogs that ran about his farms could at a pinch be mustered into a pack for hunting, at which his stablemen served as whippers-in. His grand chaplain was the village parson. Everyone called him 'My Lord', and laughed at his anecdotes.

Her ladyship the Baroness weighed about twenty-five stone. This contributed greatly to her prestige, which was enhanced by the dignity with which she did the honours of the house. The daughter, whose name was Cunégonde, was seventeen years old, fresh complexioned, plump, and attractive. The son of the house had the reputation of being 'a chip of the old block'.

The family had a household oracle, a tutor named Pangloss. Young Candide absorbed his teachings with the open-hearted simplicity of his age and nature. These teachings were metaphysico-theologo-cosmolonigological. Pangloss could prove to everybody's satisfaction that there is no effect without a cause: furthermore, that in this best of all possible worlds the Baron's castle was the finest of castles, and the Baroness the finest of all possible baronesses.

'It is demonstrable', Pangloss would say, 'that things cannot be other than they are. For, since everything is made for a purpose, everything must be for the best possible purpose. Noses, you observe, were made to support spectacles: consequently, we have spectacles. Legs, it is plain, were created to wear breeches, and are supplied with them. Stone was made to be quarried, and built into castles: that is why his lordship has such a fine castle—for the greatest baron in the province must of necessity also be the best housed. Pigs were made to be eaten: so we eat pork all the year round. It follows that those who say that *everything is good* are talking foolishly: what they should say is that *everything is for the best*.'[1]

Candide listened attentively to all this, and believed it. For his part, he thought Mistress Cunégonde extremely beautiful, though he never had the courage to tell her so. He concluded that, next to the happiness of being born a Baron von Thunder-ten-Tronckh, the second degree of happiness was to be Mistress Cunégonde; the third, to see

---

[1] In the French, 'tout est bien' and 'tout est au mieux'. This is the only passage in which Voltaire seems to indicate that there is any contradiction between the two phrases. Elsewhere Pangloss uses both as expressions of his doctrine, apparently almost interchangeably.

her every day; and the fourth, to be taught by Dr. Pangloss, the greatest philosopher in the province, and, therefore, in the whole world.

One day Cunégonde was walking near the castle, in the little copse which was known as 'the park', when through the bushes she saw Dr. Pangloss giving a lesson in applied physics to her mother's maid, a pretty and obliging little brunette. Having an inborn passion for natural science, Cunégonde, without betraying her presence, watched the Doctor's repeated demonstrations. She had no difficulty in understanding his 'sufficing reason'—a phrase that he often used—or the sequence of causes and effects. She returned home in a state of pensive agitation, filled with a desire for knowledge and reflecting that she herself might well become young Candide's 'sufficing reason'—and vice versa.

On her way back to the castle, she met Candide. She blushed, and greeted him in a faltering voice. Candide blushed too, and spoke without knowing what he said.

Next day, as they were leaving the table after dinner, Cunégonde and Candide found themselves behind a screen. Cunégonde dropped her handkerchief, and Candide picked it up. She artlessly seized his hand, and the youth artlessly kissed hers—with remarkable warmth, intensity and grace. Their lips met, their eyes sparkled, their knees trembled, their hands strayed . . .

Baron von Thunder-ten-Tronckh, who happened to pass by the screen, observed this interplay of cause and effect. He drove Candide out of the castle, with vigorous kicks from behind. Cunégonde fainted, and on coming to was smacked by the Baroness. There was consternation in the finest and best of all possible castles.

CHAPTER II

RUNNING THE GAUNTLET

EXPELLED from his earthly paradise, Candide wandered blindly and in tears, casting his eyes towards Heaven, or back towards the finest of castles, where lay the loveliest of barons' daughters. He lay down to sleep in a furrow; it was snowing heavily.

Next day, numb with cold, he dragged himself to the nearest village, which was called Valdberghofftrarbkdikdorff. Penniless and faint with hunger and fatigue, he loitered gloomily at the door of an inn.

He was observed by two men dressed in blue. 'Comrade,' said one of these, 'yonder is a well-made young fellow—of the right height, too.' They came up to Candide, and politely invited him to dine with them. 'Gentlemen,' said Candide, 'I am much honoured, but I have not the money for my share.'

'My dear young gentleman,' said one of the blue-coats, 'persons of your build and quality never pay for anything. Let me see, now, I reckon you would be five feet five inches high?'

'Yes, sirs, that is exactly my height', Candide bowed.

'Well, then, young gentleman, pray sit down with us. We will not only pay your reckoning, but will never suffer a man like you to want money. Men were born to assist one another.'

'You are perfectly right', said Candide. 'That is what Dr. Pangloss always says. I now see clearly that everything is for the best.'

His companions pressed several crowns upon him. He accepted, offering in exchange an I.O.U., which they declined to take. 'You are, I'll be bound, a man of loyalty and devotion?' said one of them.

'Yes, indeed, Mistress Cunégonde has all my ——'

'No, no, what we mean is, are you not loyally devoted to the King of Bulgaria?'

'Why, not at all, since I have never seen him.'

'But 'tis the most charming of kings! Come, we must drink to his health.' Candide drank to the toast.

'That's all that is required', he was then informed. 'You are now a mainstay, defender and hero of the Bulgarian people. Your fortune is made, you are on the high road to glory.'

Thereupon the two blue-coats put Candide in irons, and led him off to their regiment. He was taught to right turn, left turn, draw his rammer, return his rammer, present, fire, double quick march, and received thirty strokes with a cane. Next day he drilled a little less badly, and received only twenty strokes. On the third day he earned the admiration of his comrades by receiving only ten.

Candide was bewildered, and could not see how he was a hero. One fine spring day he decided to go for a walk—not to any place in particular—acting on the principle that human beings, like animals, have the right to use their legs as they wish. He had gone less than two leagues when he was overtaken by four other heroes, six feet tall, who tied him up and carried him to a prison cell.

At the court-martial, Candide was asked whether he preferred to run the gauntlet thirty-six times through the whole regiment, or to have his skull split by a dozen bullets. It was no use his saying that he didn't want either. He had to choose; so he exercised that divine gift known as 'Free Will' by choosing to run the gauntlet thirty-six times.

He performed two of these canters. Since the regiment numbered two thousand men, this meant four thousand rammer blows, which laid his muscles and nerves bare from the neck to the rump.

As they were getting ready for the third lap, Candide gave up, and asked them, as a favour, to blow his brains out. The favour was granted. His eyes were bandaged, and he was told to kneel down.

At this moment the King of Bulgaria happened to pass by, and asked what the culprit had done. Being told, and being a monarch of genius, he realized that Candide was simply an unworldly young metaphysician, and pardoned him—for which act of clemency this king will no doubt be celebrated in all the newspapers and for all time.

A worthy surgeon healed Candide's wounds in three weeks, with salves originally prescribed by Dioscorides. By the time he had some of his skin back, and was able to walk, the King of Bulgaria was at war with the King of Abaria.

CHAPTER III

ESCAPE INTO HOLLAND

THE two armies were unrivalled for smartness of drill and turn-out, excellence of equipment and soundness of tactical disposition. Their trumpets, fifes, hautboys, drums and cannon made a music never heard in hell itself.

To start with, the artillery laid low about six thousand men on either side. After that, musket fire rid this best of all possible worlds of some nine to ten thousand of the scum of its surface. Finally, the bayonet was 'sufficing reason' for the deaths of some thousands more. The total number of deaths may have been about thirty thousand.

Candide shuddered, as a philosopher well might, and did his best to hide himself during the heroic butchery. At length—whilst, on the orders of the two kings, the *Te Deum* was being sung in both camps—he decided to go and continue his meditations on the nature of cause and effect in some other part of the world.

Passing over heaps of dead and dying, he came to a neighbouring village. It was in ashes, having been an Abarian village and therefore burnt, in accordance with the laws of war, by the Bulgarians. Old men mangled by bayonets watched their wives dying with gashes in their throats, clasping their children to their blood-stained breasts. Amongst the dying were girls who had been used to satisfy a number of heroes' natural needs, and had afterwards been disembowelled. Other women, half burnt alive, begged to be put out of their pain. The ground was covered with brains, arms and legs.

As fast as he could, Candide made off to another village. This one was Bulgarian, and the Abarian heroes had treated it in the same way.

Treading upon quivering limbs and rubble, Candide at length emerged from the theatre of war. His thoughts were still full of Mistress Cunégonde.

He had a small quantity of food in his haversack; but this had given out by the time he reached Holland. He had heard, however, that all the people of this country were rich, and expected to be as well treated there as he had been in the Baron's castle, up to the moment when Cunégonde's beauty had caused his expulsion.

He begged from several substantial-looking citizens, who told him that if he continued in this occupation he would be sent to a house of correction, to teach him how to live properly. At length he spoke to a man who, as it happened, had just been addressing a large gathering for over an hour on the subject of charity. The orator eyed him askance, and inquired: 'What brought you hither? Are you for the good cause?'

'Indeed, sir,' Candide answered shyly, 'I conceive that there can be no effect without a cause. Everything is bound upon a chain of necessity, and is arranged for the best. It was necessary that I should be driven from the presence of Mistress Cunégonde, and should run the gauntlet. Now it is necessary for me to beg my bread, until I can earn it. All this could not have been otherwise.'

'Hark ye, friend, do you hold the Pope to be anti-Christ?'

'I have never heard anyone say so. But whether he be or no, I am hungry.'

'Thou dost not deserve to eat. Hence, scoundrel! Away, wretch! Come not near me, for thy life!'

The orator's wife had been looking out of a window overhead. Seeing a man who doubted whether the Pope was anti-Christ, she emptied a chamberpot upon his head— an example of the excesses to which women are driven by religious zeal.

A man who had never been baptized, a kindly Anabaptist named James, witnessed this cruel and ignominious treatment of a fellow-man—a poor creature with two legs and a soul—and took Candide to his house, cleaned him up and gave him food and beer. Afterwards he gave him two florins, and even offered to teach him the trade of weaving Persian textiles—which, as it happens, are also manufactured in Holland.

Candide fell at James's feet, and exclaimed: 'My master Pangloss was in the right. Everything in this world is for the best. 'Tis plainly so, for I am much more affected by your generosity than I was by the harshness of the gentleman in the black cloak and his wife.'

CHAPTER IV

PANGLOSS ON THE POX

NEXT day, whilst out for a walk, Candide met a beggar covered with sores. The man's eyes were sunk in his head, the end of his nose eaten away, his mouth awry, his teeth black. He spoke in a husky whisper, coughed violently, and seemed to spit out a tooth at every spasm.

Candide felt even more pity than revulsion. He gave the horrible mendicant the two florins he had received from the Anabaptist; and then recoiled in dismay, as the apparition, gazing at him, burst into tears and fell on his neck.

'Alas,' said the poor creature, 'don't you know your poor Pangloss?'

'What, can it be you, my dear master—and in so fearful a plight? What disaster has befallen you? Why have you left the finest of castles? What is become of Mistress Cunégonde, that pearl amongst young ladies, that masterpiece of nature?'

'I am utterly spent', said Pangloss. Candide led him to the Anabaptist's stable, where he brought him something to eat. When Pangloss was feeling better, Candide resumed his questions: 'And now, pray, what of Cunégonde?'

'She is dead.'

Candide fainted. His friend rubbed his forehead with some stale vinegar which happened to be in the stable, and he reopened his eyes. 'Cunégonde dead! Ah, where is the best of worlds now? But of what illness did she die? Was it for grief upon seeing her father kick me out of the castle?'

'Bulgarian soldiers ravished her, and afterwards ripped open her belly. Her father sought to defend her, and they broke his skull. The Baroness was cut in pieces. My poor

9

pupil was treated in exactly the same way as his sister. As for the castle, not one stone stands upon another. Not a barn remains, not a sheep, not a duck, not a tree.

'But we have had our revenge; for the Abarians have done the same in a neighbouring barony, which belonged to a Bulgarian lord.'

Candide fainted again. When he once more came to his senses, he inquired what causes and effects, what 'sufficing reason' had reduced Pangloss to his present piteous condition.

'Alas,' said Pangloss, 'it was love; love, the comfort of the human race, preserver of the universe, the soul of all feeling creatures; the tender passion of love.'

'Ah me,' said Candide, 'I too have known this love, sovereign of hearts, soul of our souls. All it brought me was one kiss, and a score of kicks on the backside. But how could so fair a cause produce in you so foul an effect?'

'Well, my dear Candide, you will remember Paquette, that pretty wench who waited on our august Baroness. In her arms I tasted those pleasures of paradise that produced the hellish torments with which you see me devoured. She suffered from an infection, and is perhaps now dead of it. She had it as a gift of a learned Franciscan friar, who derived it from the very fountain-head, since he had it of an old countess, who had it of a captain of horse, who had it of a marchioness, who had it of a page, who had it of a Jesuit, who, while yet a novice, had it in a direct line from one of the fellow-adventurers of Christopher Columbus.

'For my part, I shall give it to nobody, for I am dying.'

'Ah, Pangloss, what a sorry genealogy is that which you have described! Surely the devil was the root of it.'

'Not at all', replied the great man. 'It was a thing unavoidable, a necessary ingredient in the best of worlds; for if Columbus had not caught in an American isle this disease which poisons the spring of generation, and often even stops it, and is thus in itself evidently contrary to the great aim of nature, we should have neither chocolate nor cochineal.

'It is also to be observed that hitherto this malady is, like religious controversy, peculiar to our continent. The Turks, Indians, Persians, Chinese, Siamese and Japanese are not yet acquainted with it. There is, however, no doubt a sufficing reason why they, in their turn, should make its acquaintance within a few centuries.

'In the meantime, it is making amazing progress amongst us, and especially amongst those great and glorious armies that determine the fate of nations. One may safely affirm that, when two armies of 30,000 men each meet in battle, about 20,000 on either side have the pox.'

'That is all very interesting,' said Candide; 'but we must have you cured.'

'But how? I have not a penny, my friend, and nowhere on the surface of the globe can a man be bled or clystered without paying, or being paid for by another.'

Candide thereupon threw himself upon the mercy of the charitable Anabaptist James, and painted to him so striking a picture of his friend's condition that the good man at once took Dr. Pangloss into his house and paid for treatment for him. The result was that Pangloss lost only one eye and one ear. Since he wrote a good hand and was an excellent arithmetician, James made him his bookkeeper.

Two months later, James had to go on business to Lisbon, and took the two philosophers with him.

On the voyage, Pangloss explained to James the perfection of the scheme of things. James disagreed: 'Men must have deviated somewhat from their original innocence', he said. 'They were not born wolves, but they are become wolves. God did not give them twenty-four pounders nor bayonets, but they have made these things for their own destruction. I might also speak of bankruptcies, and the law which seizes upon the property of bankrupts solely in order to keep it from the creditors.'

'All that had to be', replied the one-eyed doctor. 'Private ills make up the general good. It therefore follows that, the more numerous the private ills, the greater the general good.'

As he spoke, the sky was darkening and a high wind was rising. The ship, which was now within sight of Lisbon harbour, was struck by a terrible storm.

CHAPTER V

THE DEATH OF THE ANABAPTIST

HALF of the passengers were so weak—torn by the abominable pangs that the rolling of a vessel shoots through the body's nerves and humours, which seem to clash together—that they could pay no heed to the danger. The other half screamed or prayed. The sails were in shreds, the mast broken, the ship gashed open. All efforts were useless, since no orders could be heard or given.

The Anabaptist, who was on deck trying to help, was knocked down by a frantic sailor, who himself was carried overboard, head first, by the force of his blow. His breeches caught on a broken mast, from which he dangled until James helped him back on board. James, in turn, was precipitated overboard by his effort, and fell into the sea in full view of the sailor, who calmly left him to drown.

Candide came on deck at this moment, and, seeing his benefactor going under for the third time, wanted to jump in after him; but he was restrained by Dr. Pangloss, who cogently argued that Lisbon roads had been specially contrived so that the Anabaptist might drown in them.

Whilst Pangloss was proving this point *a priori*, the ship broke up. Everyone was drowned except Pangloss, Candide and the brutal sailor. The latter swam to the shore, to which Pangloss and Candide were carried on a plank.

When they had recovered a little, they walked towards Lisbon. They still had some money, and hoped, having escaped from the storm, also to save themselves from starvation. Grieving for the death of their benefactor, they arrived at the outskirts of the city. At this moment the earth shook,[1] the sea rose up foaming in the harbour and dashed to pieces the ships lying at anchor. The streets and squares were filled with whirling masses of flame and cinders. The houses collapsed, the roofs crashing down on the shattered foundations. Thirty thousand inhabitants were crushed beneath the ruins.

The sailor whistled, and let out an oath. 'There's something to be got here', he remarked.

'What can be the sufficing reason for this phenomenon?' Pangloss wondered.

''Tis the day of judgment!' Candide exclaimed.

Risking death, the sailor dashed into the ruins in search of plunder. He found what he sought, got drunk, slept it off and then purchased the favours of the first obliging young woman he met—all this in the midst of ruined buildings and dead and dying people. Pangloss plucked his sleeve. 'Friend,' he said, 'this is not right. You trespass against the universal reason, and abuse your time.'

'Death and ounds!' the man replied. 'I am a sailor, and born in Batavia. In four voyages to Japan I have four times

[1] There was an earthquake, in which nearly 20,000 people were killed, at Lisbon on 1 November 1755.

trampled on the crucifix.[1] To the devil with you and your "universal reason"!'

Candide had been injured by flying stones, and was lying in the street covered with rubble. 'Alas!' he said to Pangloss, 'get me a little wine and oil, for I am dying.'

'This trembling of the earth's crust is no new thing', said Pangloss. 'The city of Lima, in America, experienced the same last year. Similar causes, similar effects. No doubt a subterranean train of sulphur stretches from Lima to Lisbon.'

''Tis very probable—but, for God's sake, a little oil and wine!'

'Probable! I maintain that the thing is proven.'

Candide fainted, and Pangloss brought him some water from a fountain near by.

Next day they found some food amongst the ruins, and, feeling rather stronger, joined in the work of giving aid to the survivors. Some of the citizens whom they had helped invited them to dinner. It was as good a meal as could be managed in the circumstances. The diners sat weeping over their plates, whilst Pangloss consoled them by explaining that things could not be otherwise. 'All this is for the best,' he said; 'since, if there is a volcanic eruption at Lisbon, then it could not have occurred in any other spot. It is impossible that things should be elsewhere than where they are; for everything is good.'

A little man dressed in black, who happened to be an agent of the Inquisition, was sitting next to Pangloss. 'It appears, sir,' he said suavely, 'that you do not believe in original sin; for, if everything is for the best, there can have been no fall or punishment of mankind.'

'I humbly beg your Excellency's pardon. The fall of man,

[1] In the seventeenth century, if a European shipmaster wished to enter a Japanese port, he and his crew were obliged to trample on a crucifix and declare that they were not Christians.

and the curse upon him, entered as a necessary part into the best of all possible worlds.'

'Then, sir, you do not believe in Free Will?'

'Your Excellency will excuse me. Free Will can subsist together with absolute necessity; for it was necessary that we should be free; for, indeed, the Determination of Will . . .'

The agent nodded to his henchman, who was pouring him out a glass of port.

CHAPTER VI

AN AUTO-DA-FÉ

AFTER the earthquake, which destroyed three-quarters of Lisbon, the country's leading thinkers decided that the best way of avoiding total destruction of the city was to give the people an *auto-da-fé*. The University of Coimbra was of the opinion that an infallible receipt for the prevention of earthquakes is the sight of some individuals being burnt over a slow fire.[1]

Amongst those arrested for the purpose was a Biscayan convicted of marrying his godmother, and two Portuguese who, whilst eating a chicken, had put the bacon that went with it on the edges of their plates. After dinner Dr. Pangloss and his disciple Candide were put in handcuffs: the former for what he had said, and the latter for having listened with an air of approval. They were led off to separate apartments—very cool ones, where they were in no danger of sunstroke.

A week later they were dressed in the Benedictine cassocks that are customary on such occasions, and paper mitres

[1] An auto-da-fé was held in Lisbon on 20 June 1756.

were put on their heads. Candide's cassock and mitre were painted with flames pointing downwards, and with devils that had no tails or claws; Pangloss's devils, on the other hand, had both these things, and his flames stood upright. They were led in a procession, and heard a very eloquent sermon, followed by an anthem sung in the *faux-bourdon* style of harmony. Candide was rhythmically flogged, in time to the singing. The Biscayan and the two men who did not like bacon were burnt. Pangloss was hanged—an unusual procedure at such ceremonies.

The same day there was another terrible earthquake.

Horrified, dumbfounded, bewildered, bleeding and gasping, Candide asked himself: 'If this is the best of all possible worlds, what can the others be like?' His own flogging he could bear with equanimity—he had suffered the same with the Bulgarians. But the hanging, for no comprehensible reason, of his beloved Pangloss, that greatest of philosophers; the drowning, in the very harbour, of the Anabaptist James, that best of men; and the evisceration of Mistress Cunégonde, that pearl amongst maidens: these were events whose necessity he could not understand.

As he was tottering feebly away from the place where he had been preached at, flogged, absolved and given benediction, an old woman came up to him and said: 'Be of good cheer, child, and follow me'.

CHAPTER VII

CUNÉGONDE RE-FOUND

CANDIDE was not at all of good cheer, but he followed the old woman. She led him to a hovel, where she gave him a pot of ointment, food and drink, and showed him to a clean little bed, beside which hung a suit of clothes. 'Eat, drink and sleep,' she said, 'and may Our Lady of Atocha, his lordship St. Anthony of Padua and his lordship St. James of Compostella watch over you. I shall be back tomorrow.'

Candide, who was still dazed by all that he had seen and suffered, and still more so by the old woman's kindness, sought to kiss her hand. 'It is not *my* hand you should kiss', she said. 'I shall be back tomorrow. Anoint your back, eat and sleep.'

Despite all his sorrows, Candide ate and slept. Next morning the old woman brought him breakfast, examined his back and rubbed it herself with another ointment. Later she brought him dinner and supper. The day after, she again brought him dinner. Candide kept on questioning her: who was she, what was the reason for all her kindness, how could he show his gratitude? But she did not answer.

On the evening of the second day, the old woman again came to Candide's room, but this time brought no supper. 'Come with me,' she said, 'and do not speak a word.' Taking him by the arm, she led him about a quarter of a mile into the country, to a lonely house surrounded by gardens and canals.

A small door was opened to her knock, and she led Candide by some back stairs to a small, gilt room, where she left him sitting on a brocaded sofa. Candide felt that his whole past life had been a nightmare, and that the present was also a dream, but a pleasant one.

In a short time the old woman came back, supporting a trembling young lady of majestic build, richly bejewelled and wearing a veil.

'Take off her veil', the old woman said, and Candide shyly did so. To his amazement, it was—yes, indeed, it was!—Mistress Cunégonde! He fell speechless at her feet,

17

whilst she fell backwards upon the sofa. The old woman sprinkled them copiously with spirits, and they recovered enough composure to speak. At first they could utter only broken phrases, interrupting each other's questions and answers, gasping, weeping and exclaiming. The old woman advised them to make less noise, and left them alone.

'So it is really you,' said Candide, 'alive, and here in Portugal! So they did not ravish you, they did not rip your belly open?'

'Indeed they did', said Cunégonde. 'But these two accidents are not always mortal.'

'But were your father and mother killed?'

'Alas, it is but too true!' She wept.

'And your brother?'

'Yes, he too.'

'And how came you to Portugal? And how did you know that I was here? By what strange adventure did you contrive to have me brought to this house?'

'I will tell you the whole story. But first you must tell me what has befallen you, ever since the day when you gave me that innocent little kiss, and my father kicked you out of the castle.'

Candide made devoted haste to obey her. He was still in a state of bewilderment, and also somewhat distraught by the pain of his back, so that he spoke in a quavering whisper. He gave her a straightforward account of all that had happened to him since their separation. Cunégonde kept turning up her eyes in horror. She wept to hear of the death of the Anabaptist. Then she told her own story, whilst Candide avidly listened and gazed upon her.

CHAPTER VIII

CUNÉGONDE'S STORY

'I WAS fast asleep in bed when it pleased Heaven to send the Bulgarians to our castle. They slit the throats of my father and brother, and cut my mother in pieces. I fainted at the sight, and a strapping Bulgarian, six feet high, took the opportunity to ravish me.

'This brought me to my senses. I screamed, I struggled, I bit, I scratched, I would have torn the Bulgarian's eyes out. I did not know at this time that what was happening in my father's castle was all in accordance with the laws of war. The brute thrust a knife into my left side—I still bear the scar.'

'Alas, do let me see it!' said Candide ingenuously.

'You shall; but let me proceed.'

'Pray do.'

'A Bulgarian captain came into the room. He saw me lying there bleeding, and the soldier calmly continuing his operation. Angered by the man's failure to rise to his feet and salute, the captain killed him upon my body. He then had my wound dressed, and carried me, prisoner of war, to his quarters.

'I washed his few shirts and cooked his meals. I must confess that he thought me mighty handsome, and I shall not deny that he himself was very well made, with a white, smooth skin. For the rest, he was a dull man, with little knowledge of philosophy—not at all like a pupil of Dr. Pangloss.

'Three months later the captain had grown tired of me. Having lost all his money at play, he sold me to a Jew named Don Issachar, who traded to Holland and Portugal, and was passionately fond of women. This Jew took a great liking for my person, but could not prevail over it. I resisted him better than I had resisted the Bulgarian soldier. A chaste woman may be ravished once, but her virtue is all the stronger for it.

'To tame me to his desires, the Jew then brought me to this place. I had believed that nothing could equal the beauty of Thunder-ten-Tronckh, but my eyes have been opened.

'One day, while at Mass, I was observed by the Grand Inquisitor. He ogled me throughout the service, and afterwards sent me a message that he wished to speak with me on private business. I was led to his palace, where I told him my origin. He represented to me how much beneath my rank it was to belong to an Israelite, and sent an intermediary to Don Issachar with the proposal that he should yield me to his lordship.

'Don Issachar, who is a court banker and a man of standing, refused to do anything of the sort, and the Inquisitor threatened him with an *auto-da-fé*. The upshot was that my Jew came to a composition, whereby this house and myself should belong to the two of them jointly. The Jew was to be the owner on Tuesday, Thursday and the Jewish Sabbath, the Inquisitor on the other days of the week.

'This arrangement has been in force for six months, but not without disputes; for they often fail to agree as to whether the night from Saturday to Sunday comes under the old law or the new. For my part, I have hitherto withstood both of them—and that, I think, is the reason why they still love me.

'It came about that, in order to avert the scourge of the earthquakes, and also to intimidate Don Issachar, my Lord Inquisitor was pleased to hold an *auto-da-fé*. He did me the honour of inviting me to be present, and I had a very good seat. In the interval between Mass and the executions, the ladies were served with refreshments.

'I assure you that I was dreadfully shocked at the burning

of the two Jews, and of that poor Biscayan who had married his godmother. But what was my amazement and horror when I saw, in Benedictine cassock and mitre, a figure resembling Pangloss! I rubbed my eyes, gazed at him closely, and saw him hanged. I swooned away.

'Scarce had I recovered my senses, when I beheld you stripped naked. That was the height of my horror, consternation, grief and despair. I will confess to you that your skin is even whiter and more blooming than that of my Bulgarian captain. The sight enhanced the pangs of grief that were crushing and gnawing at me. I shrieked, I wanted to cry out: "Hold, barbarians!" But my voice failed me, and in any case it would have done no good.

'After your flogging, I said to myself: "To think that my dear Candide and wise old Pangloss should be here in Lisbon, the one to receive a hundred lashes and the other to be hanged, and all on the orders of my Lord Inquisitor—and he my suitor! 'Twas a cruel lie that Pangloss told me when he said that everything in this world is for the best!"

'Agitated and bewildered, now in a frenzy and now half dead with weakness, I kept thinking of the massacre of my father, mother and brother; of the insolence of that villainous Bulgarian soldier and the wound he dealt me; of my servitude and employment as a cook-wench; of my wretched Don Issachar and horrible Inquisitor; of that swelling *Miserere* that was sung while you were being flogged; and especially, again and again, of that kiss you gave me behind the screen, on the day I saw you for the last time.

'I praised God for bringing you back to me after so many trials, and ordered my old attendant to take care of you and to bring you hither as soon as she might. She has carried out my orders well, and I have the inexpressible delight of seeing you again.

'But you must be ravening with hunger; and I, too, have a great appetite. Let us first have supper.'

They sat down at table, and after supper returned to the magnificent sofa already mentioned. They were still there when Don Issachar entered. It was the Sabbath day, and he had come to exercise his rights and expatiate upon his tender passion.

CHAPTER IX

DEATHS OF THE JEW AND THE INQUISITOR

ISSACHAR was the quickest-tempered Hebrew since the Babylonian captivity. 'How now, thou Galilean bitch!' he said. 'Is not the Inquisitor enough for thee, that I must also share thee with this rascal? He drew a long poniard, which he always carried, and rushed at Candide, thinking him to be unarmed. But the stalwart young Westphalian had received, along with the suit of clothes that the old woman gave him, an excellent sword. Despite his naturally gentle and peaceable nature, he drew, and laid the Israelite stone dead at the fair Cunégonde's feet.

'Holy Virgin!' she cried. 'What will become of us? A man killed in my apartment! If the peace-officers come, we are undone!'

'Had Pangloss not been hanged,' Candide replied, 'that great philosopher would have given us good advice in this emergency. Since we have not him, let us consult the old woman.'

She was a shrewd old lady, and very willing to give advice. As she was doing so, the door again opened. It was an hour after midnight, and therefore the beginning of Sunday, a day which belonged to my Lord Inquisitor. He was now confronted with Candide, that recently flogged felon, standing with drawn sword; a corpse on the ground; Cunégonde cowering with fright; and the old woman giving her advice.

The train of thought that now passed clearly and rapidly through Candide's mind ran as follows: 'If this holy man calls for assistance, he will certainly have me burnt, and perhaps Cunégonde too. He has had me cruelly whipped. He is my rival. I have set out on a career of slaughter. There is no time to hesitate.' Before the Inquisitor could recover from his surprise, Candide ran him through the body, and laid him beside the Jew.

'And now there's another of them!' wailed Cunégonde. 'This is unpardonable, we are excommunicated, our last hour is come! But how could you—you, who are of so mild a temper—bring yourself to kill a Jew and a prelate, all in two minutes?'

'Beautiful Mistress,' said Candide, 'when a man is in love, is jealous, and has been flogged by the Inquisition, he does the most surprising things.'

'There are three Andalusian horses in the stable,' said the old woman, 'with their saddles and bridles. Let Candide make them ready. Madam has some moidores and diamonds. Let us get quickly to horse—though, for my part, I have only one buttock to sit upon—and be off to Cadiz. The weather is as fine as could be, and 'tis a great pleasure to travel in the cool of the night.'

Candide at once saddled the three horses, and they covered thirty miles without stopping. Meanwhile the Holy Brotherhood entered Issachar's house, buried his lordship in a fine church, and threw Issachar on a dunghill.

By this time Candide, Cunégonde and the old woman were already at an inn in the little town of Aracena, in the Sierra Morena, where they were engaged in an earnest discussion.

CHAPTER X

EMBARKATION FOR THE NEW WORLD

CUNÉGONDE wept. 'Who can have taken them?' she said. 'What shall we live on? What are we to do?' Her moidores and diamonds had disappeared. 'Where can I find a Jew or an Inquisitor to give me some more?' she sobbed.

'I strongly suspect a certain reverend Franciscan friar', said the old woman. 'He lay last night in the same inn with us at Badajoz. God preserve me from making hasty judgments, but he came into our room twice, and left the inn long before us.'

'Ah me,' said Candide, 'Pangloss often used to demonstrate that the world's goods are common to all men, and that each has an equal right to them. But, even according to this principle, the friar should have left us enough to carry us to the end of our journey. Have you nothing left at all, dearest Cunégonde?'

'Not a stiver.'

'Then what is our course of action?'

'Sell one of the horses', said the old woman. 'I will ride on the crupper behind Mistress Cunégonde, though I have only one buttock to ride on, and we shall reach Cadiz.'

A Benedictine prior who was lodging at the inn bought the horse very cheap. They rode through Lucena, Chillas and Lebrija, and arrived at Cadiz.

Here a fleet was being equipped, and troops raised, to teach a lesson to the reverend Jesuit Fathers of Paraguay. The Jesuits were accused of having stirred up one of their Indian tribes, in the area of San Sacramento, to revolt against the Kings of Spain and Portugal.

Profiting from his service with the Bulgarians, Candide

went through the drill of that army in the presence of the Spanish general. He displayed so much smartness, speed, initiative, morale and efficiency that he was given command of a company. Thus, as a captain, he was able to take on board with him Cunégonde, the old woman, two valets and the Grand Inquisitor's horses.

During the voyage they spent much time discussing poor Pangloss's doctrines. 'We are going to another world,' said Candide, 'and doubtless it is in this new world that everything is good; for I must confess that events in the world we have known, both physical and spiritual, have been enough to make one tremble a little.'

'I love you with all my heart', said Cunégonde. 'But nonetheless I am still scared to the depths of my soul by all that I have seen and undergone.'

'All will be well. Why, the seas of this new world are already better than the seas of Europe. They are smoother, and the winds are steadier. For certain, it is this new world that will prove to be the best of all possible ones.'

'God grant it. But I have been so horribly unhappy in the world I have known, that my heart is almost shut against hope.'

'You moan and complain,' said the old woman, 'but you have not suffered half what I have done.'

Cunégonde could hardly help laughing at this seemingly ridiculous assertion. 'My good dame,' she said, 'unless you have been ravished by two Bulgarians—stabbed in the stomach twice over—seen two of your castles demolished, two mothers and two fathers having their throats cut, and two lovers flogged at an *auto-da-fé*—I do not see how you can claim to have endured twice as much misery as I have. Add to this, that I was born a baroness, with seventy-two quarterings, and have since been a cook-wench.'

'Mistress, I have never told you my origin. And if I were to show you my backside, you would not speak so hastily.'

Cunégonde and Candide were eager to know what the old woman meant. She told them her story as follows.

CHAPTER XI

THE OLD WOMAN'S STORY—1

'My eyes were not always bloodshot and red-rimmed; my nose did not always touch my chin; nor was I always a servant.

'I am the daughter of Pope Urban X[1] and the Princess of Palestrina. Until the age of fourteen I was brought up in a castle to which none of the castles of your German princes would serve as stables. A single one of my robes was worth more than all the treasure in Westphalia.

'I grew in beauty, grace and talent, in the midst of pleasures, homage and fair expectations. Already I inspired men with love. Already my bosom was forming—and what a bosom! White, firm and shaped like that of the Venus of the Medicis. My eyebrows were black, my eyes flashed brighter than the stars—or so our poets told me. The women who dressed and undressed me fell into ecstasies when they beheld me before and behind; and all the men would willingly have changed places with them.

'I was betrothed to a ruling Prince of Massa Carrara. Such a prince! As handsome as myself, crammed full of sweetness and charm, brilliantly witty and aflame with love. I loved him as one loves for the first time—with idolatrous fervour.

[1] 'Observe the extreme discretion of the author. There has until now been no Pope named Urban X. The author is unwilling to attribute a bastard to any known Pope. What circumspection! What delicacy of conscience!'—*Note by Voltaire.*

'The nuptials were to be of unprecedented pomp and magnificence, with festivities, roundabouts and light operas. All Italy composed sonnets in my praise—all of them execrable. The moment of my supreme happiness was at hand, when an old marquesa, who had been my prince's mistress, invited him to take chocolate with her. He died less than two hours later, in frightful convulsions.

'But that was a mere trifle. My mother, who was in despair, although her affliction was less than mine, resolved to remove herself for a while from the scene of tragedy. She had a fine estate near Gaeta, for which we embarked on a galley gilt, in the fashion of my country, like the high altar of St. Peter's at Rome. In our passage we were boarded by a Sali corsair. Our men fought like soldiers of the Pope—that is, they flung themselves on their knees, laid down their arms and begged the corsair to give them absolution *in articulo mortis*.

'They were forthwith stripped as naked as apes; as also were my mother, our maids of honour and myself. It is amazing how expert these gentry are at undressing people. But what astonished me more was that they thrust their fingers into a region where we women as a rule allow only —— to enter. At first I thought this very strange—it is remarkable how travel broadens the mind—but I later learnt that the purpose was to discover if we had concealed any diamonds. The practice has been established from time immemorial among the highly efficient nations that scour the seas. I have been told that the religious Knights of Malta never neglect it when they capture Turks of either sex. It is a part of the law of nations, from which they never deviate.

'I need not tell you how hard it is for a young princess and her mother to be led off to slavery in Morocco. You can likewise imagine what we had to suffer on board the corsair. My mother was still very handsome, and our maids

27

of honour, and even our common waiting women, had more charms than are to be found in all Africa. As to myself, I was enchanting; I was beauty and grace itself—and I was a maid. I did not remain one long; the flower that had been reserved for the Prince of Massa Carrara was snatched from me by the corsair captain, a hideous negro, who positively thought that he was doing me an honour.

'Indeed, both the Princess of Palestrina and myself must have had very strong constitutions to withstand all that we endured till our arrival at Morocco. But I shall not waste time on further relating such commonplace matters.

'At the time of our arrival, Morocco was being deluged with blood. Fifty sons of the Emperor Muley Ishmael were each at the head of a faction. Thus fifty different civil wars were in progress—blacks against blacks, mulattoes against blacks, and mulattoes against mulattoes. The whole empire was a field of continual slaughter.

'As soon as we landed, a party of blacks of a faction hostile to that of our captain, came to take away his booty. Next to his diamonds and gold, we were the most valuable things he had. A battle ensued, such as you never see in your European climates. The northern peoples have not the hot blood, nor the raging lust after women, of the African. It seems to be milk that runs in European veins, compared with the vitriol and flame that gush through the veins of the inhabitants of Mount Atlas and the neighbouring lands. They fought with the fury of the lions, tigers and serpents of their country, to know who should have us. A Moor seized my mother by the right arm, my captain's lieutenant seized her by the left arm, another Moor took her by the right leg and one of our corsairs by the left. Almost all our women were thus torn between four men.

'My captain kept me hidden behind him, and with drawn scimitar slew all who stood in his way. The end of it was that my mother and all our Italian women were torn to pieces by the monsters who contended for them. Captives and captors, soldiers and sailors, blacks, whites and mulattoes, and lastly my captain himself, were all slain, and I was left half dead upon a heap of carcasses.

'Similar scenes were being enacted over a region more than three hundred leagues in length; yet there was never any failure to observe the five daily prayers enjoined by Mahomet.

'I disengaged myself with difficulty from the pile of bloody corpses, and dragged myself beneath a large orange tree on the bank of a near-by stream. Here I collapsed from fright, weariness, horror, despair and hunger, and my crushed senses yielded to an oblivion that was rather a swoon than a sleep.

'In this state of weakness and insensibility, between life and death, I felt myself pressed upon by something that moved up and down on my body. Opening my eyes I saw a white man, of good appearance, who was sighing and muttering: "*O che sciagura d'essere senza coglioni!*"'

CHAPTER XII

THE OLD WOMAN'S STORY—2

'ASTONISHED and delighted to hear the speech of my country, and not less surprised at the man's words, I told him that there were heavier misfortunes than what he complained of. I briefly described to him the horrors that I had passed through, and fell back into my swoon.

'The man carried me to a house, where he had me put to bed and given food. He waited on me, comforted and flattered me, vowing that he had never seen anything so beautiful as myself, and had never before so much regretted the loss of what no one could restore to him.

'"I was born at Naples," he said, "where they caponize two or three thousand children every year. Some die; others acquire voices more beautiful than women's; and others become Governors of states.[1] In my case, the operation was a great success, and I was one of the singers in the Princess of Palestrina's chapel."

'"How," cried I, "in my mother's chapel!"

'"What, is the Princess of Palestrina your mother?" he exclaimed, and burst into tears. "Then you are the little princess whom I had the care of until she was six years old. Already at that age she promised to be as beautiful as you."

'"Yes, 'tis I. My mother lies four hundred yards hence, torn in four pieces, beneath a heap of dead. . ."

'We exchanged accounts of our adventures. A certain Christian state had sent him as envoy to the King of Morocco, to conclude a treaty with that monarch whereby he was to be furnished with powder, guns and ships to help him to destroy the commerce of other Christians.[2]

'"My mission has been accomplished", said the eunuch. "I am going to take ship at Ceuta, and will escort you back to Italy. *Ma che sciagura d'essere senza coglioni!*"

'I thanked him, with tears of joy. Thereupon, instead of conducting me to Italy, he carried me to Algiers, where he sold me to the Dey.

'Soon afterwards the plague, which had made the tour of Africa, Asia and Europe, began raging in Algiers. You have seen earthquakes, mistress; but tell me, had you ever the plague?'

[1] Ferdinand VI appointed a Neapolitan eunuch named Farinelli to be a Governor in Spain.

[2] During the War of the Spanish Succession the King of Portugal sent such an envoy to Morocco.

'No', said Cunégonde.

'If you had, you would confess that an earthquake is a trifle to it—and it is very common in Africa.'

'I was one of those seized with it. Picture to yourself the plight of a Pope's daughter, fifteen years old, who within three months had suffered want and slavery, had been ravished almost daily, had seen her mother torn into four pieces, had passed through famine and war, and was now dying of the plague in Algiers!

'In the end, I did not die; but my eunuch, and the Dey, and almost the whole seraglio of Algiers, were swept off.

'When the plague had spent its first fury, a sale was made of the Dey's slaves. A merchant bought me, and carried me to Tunis. There he sold me to another merchant, by whom I was sold again at Tripoli. From Tripoli I was sold to Alexandria, thence to Smyrna, and thence to Constantinople, where I became the property of an aga of the Janissaries.

'This aga was ordered away to the defence of Azov, which was besieged by the Russians.[1] Being a great affecter of the fair sex, he took his whole seraglio with him into the field. We were lodged in a small fort upon the Maeotic Swamp, under guard of two black eunuchs and twenty soldiers.

'Our army made a great slaughter among the Russians, but they repaid us well in kind. Azov was reduced to blood and ashes; no quarter was given on grounds either of age or of sex.

'At length only our little fort was left. The enemy sought to reduce it by starvation. The twenty Janissaries, who had sworn never to surrender, were obliged to eat the two eunuchs, rather than break their oath. A few days later, they resolved to eat the women.

'We had with us a very devout imam, who in an eloquent

[1] Azov was besieged by the Russians in 1739.

sermon persuaded them not to kill us outright. "Only cut off one of the buttocks of each of these ladies," he said, "and you will find an excellent meal. If need be, you can in a few days have recourse to its fellow. Heaven will smile upon so charitable an action, and you will be relieved."

'His eloquence persuaded them, and we were subjected to this fearsome operation. The imam applied the same ointment as is used on newly circumcised children. We were all at death's door.

'Just when the Janissaries had finished the repast with which we had supplied them, the Russians attacked in flat-bottomed boats, and every single Janissary was killed.

'The Russians paid no heed to our plight. But they had with them a French surgeon—such people are found everywhere—a man of great skill, who took care of us and healed us. I shall always remember that no sooner were my wounds closed than he made advances to me. He also sought to cheer us by explaining that the like had happened in many sieges, and was in full conformity with the laws of war.

'As soon as my companions and I could walk, we were sent to Moscow. I fell to the lot of a boyar, who set me to work in his garden, and gave me twenty lashes a day. Two years later this nobleman, with some thirty others, was broken on the wheel as a result of a court feud. I took advantage of this event to escape.

'After making my way across Russia, I for a long time served as chambermaid at inns at Riga, Rostock, Wismar, Leipzig, Cassel, Utrecht, Leyden, the Hague and Rotterdam. I grew old in poverty and degradation, with only the half of a backside, and remembering always that I was a Pope's daughter. A hundred times I wished to kill myself, but my love of life persisted. This ridiculous weakness is perhaps one of the most fatal of our faults. For what could be more stupid than to go on carrying a burden that we always long to lay down? To loathe, and yet cling to, existence? In short, to cherish the serpent that devours us, until it has eaten our hearts?

'In the countries through which my destiny led me, and in the inns where I served, I saw a prodigious number of people who hated their existence. Yet only twelve of them voluntarily put an end to it: namely, three negroes, four Englishmen, four Genevans and a German professor named Robeck.

'My last place was with the Jew, Don Issachar, who set me to attend upon you, my fair lady. I have attached myself to your fortunes, and have been more concerned with your adventures than with my own. I should not have even spoken to you of my mishaps had you not provoked me a little, and were it not customary on shipboard to pass the time by telling stories.

'In short, mistress, I know much of the world. Divert yourself by inducing each passenger to tell you his story; and if there is a single one of them who has not many times cursed his life, and sworn that he was the most wretched of men, I give you leave to throw me head foremost into the sea.'

CHAPTER XIII

THE GOVERNOR OF BUENOS AIRES

AFTER hearing the old woman's story Cunégonde paid her the respect due to a person of her rank and merits. On her suggestion, she induced all the passengers, one after another, to relate their adventures; and she and Candide had to admit that the old woman was right.

''Tis a sad pity,' said Candide, 'that wise old Pangloss was hanged—and how such a thing could happen at an *auto-da-fé*, I don't know—since he might have discoursed to us admirably on the physical and moral evils that overspread the earth and sea; and I should have been bold enough to offer some few respectful objections.'

On reaching Buenos Aires, Cunégonde, Captain Candide and the old woman paid a visit to the Governor. He was called Don Fernando d'Ibarro y Figueora y Mascarenes y Lampourdos y Souza, and his behaviour befitted a man with so many names. In conversation with men, his air of noble disdain, uptilted nose, excruciatingly affected accent and stilted manner made everyone long to hit him. For women he had an insatiable passion.

Cunégonde seemed to the Governor the most beautiful thing he had ever seen. He inquired whether she was the Captain's wife. His manner alarmed Candide, who dared not say that she was his wife—since she was not; nor that she was his sister—since she was not that either. Although a useful lie of this sort would have had many historical precedents, Candide was too open-hearted for such deceit. 'Mistress Cunégonde', he said, 'intends to do me the honour to marry me—and we beg your Excellency to condescend to grace the ceremony with your presence.'

Don Fernando d'Ibarro y Figueora y Mascarenes y Lampourdos y Souza twirled his moustache, smiled sourly and ordered Captain Candide to go and inspect his company. Left alone with Cunégonde, he declared his passion, and swore that he would marry her next day—in church or otherwise, her beauty was such that it was all one to him.

Cunégonde asked for a quarter of an hour's reflection. She wanted to ask advice of the old woman.

'Mistress,' said the old woman, 'you have seventy-two quarterings, but not a penny. If you choose, you can be the wife of the greatest nobleman in South America—with a very fine moustache, too. Is it for you to pride yourself upon an unshakable fidelity? You have been ravished by the Bulgarians. A Jew and an Inquisitor have enjoyed your favours. Misfortunes carry their own privileges. If I were you, I should have no hesitation in marrying the Governor —and making the Captain's fortune.'

That same day a small ship entered the harbour of Buenos Aires, carrying an alcayde and a party of alguazils. The reason for their arrival was as follows:

As the old woman had guessed, the thief of Cunégonde's money and jewels at Badajoz had been a Franciscan friar. This man had tried to sell some of the stones to a jeweller, who had recognized them as the property of the Grand Inquisitor. Before being hanged, the friar confessed his theft, and had described the persons whom he had robbed and the road they were taking. The flight of Cunégonde and Candide was by this time known. They were pursued to Cadiz, and thence across the ocean. The pursuing ship had now arrived in Buenos Aires harbour; and already the report had spread that it had an alcayde aboard, and had come for the murderers of his lordship the Grand Inquisitor.

The clever old woman realized the situation at once. 'You cannot run away,' she said to Cunégonde, 'and you have nothing to fear. It was not you who killed his lordship. Besides, as the Governor is in love with you, he will not suffer you to be ill-treated. Stand your ground.'

Then she hurried to Candide. 'Flee,' she said, 'or you will be burnt alive within the hour.'

He had not a moment to lose. But how could he bring himself to part from Cunégonde, and where was he to go?

CHAPTER XIV

FLIGHT TO PARAGUAY

CANDIDE had brought with him from Cadiz a valet of a type that is common along the coasts of Spain and in the colonies. He was only one quarter Spanish, having been born in Tucuman of a mestizo father. He had been at various times a choirboy, a sacristan, a sailor, a monk, a shop-boy, a soldier and a lacquey. His name was Cacambo, and he had a great affection for Candide—which, indeed, the latter well deserved.

Cacambo quickly saddled the two Andalusian horses. 'Come, master,' he said, 'let us take the old woman's advice, and be off without more ado.'

'My dearest Cunégonde,' said Candide, weeping, 'must I leave you in the very moment the Governor was going to preside at our wedding? What will become of you, so far from home?'

'She must do as well as she can', said Cacambo. 'Women can always look after themselves. God provides for them. Let us be off.'

'But whither wilt thou carry me? Where can we go? What shall we do without Cunégonde?'

'By St. James of Compostella! You were on your way to fight the Jesuits; let us fight on their side. I know the roads, and can lead you to their kingdom. They will be delighted to have a captain who knows Bulgarian drill and tactics. You will make a vast fortune. When one cannot come to terms with one world, one can always do so with another. 'Tis a great delight to see and do new things.'

'Then you have been in Paraguay?'

'Ay, marry, have I! I was a scout in the College of the Assumption, and I know the domain of *los padres* as well as I know the streets of Cadiz. And what an admirable domain it is! The kingdom is already upwards of three hundred leagues in diameter, and divided into thirty provinces. *Los padres* own everything, the tribes nothing. 'Tis a masterpiece of rational and just rule! Why, I know of nothing so near to divine Almightiness as *los padres*: here they make war against the kings of Spain and Portugal, and over in Europe they receive these same kings in their confessionals. Here they kill Spaniards, and over there they speed them on their way to Heaven: 'tis exquisite!

'But let us make haste; you have rare good fortune in store for you. How pleased *los padres* will be to learn that they are getting a captain who knows Bulgarian drill and tactics!'

When they reached the first frontier barrier, Cacambo told the outpost that a captain wished to speak with his lordship the commandant. The main guard was turned out, and a Paraguayan officer ran to kneel before the commandant and report the news to him. Candide and Cacambo were immediately disarmed, and their horses were seized. They were led, between two files, towards the commandant, who wore a three-cornered hat and a tucked-up habit, had a sword by his side and carried a half-pike. He gave a sign, and the newcomers were surrounded by twenty-four soldiers. A sergeant told them that they must wait; the commandant could not speak with them, since the Reverend Father Provincial did not allow any Spaniard to speak except in his presence, or to remain in the country for more than three hours.

'Where is the Reverend Father Provincial?' Cacambo asked.

'He has said Mass, and is on parade. You will not be able to kiss his spurs for another three hours.'

'But the Captain and I are perishing with hunger; and the Captain is no Spaniard, but a German. Could we not eat while we wait for his Reverence?'

The sergeant immediately reported what he had been told to the commandant. 'God be praised!' said the latter. 'If he is a German, I may speak with him. Let him be brought to my arbour.'

Candide was conducted to a bower adorned with a

pretty colonnade of green and yellow marble, and with cages containing parrots, humming-birds, guinea-fowl, and birds of other rare kinds. An excellent breakfast was waiting in gold vessels. Whilst his Paraguayan troops ate maize from wooden trenchers in the blazing sun, the Reverend Father Commandant entered the arbour.

He was a very handsome young man, round-faced, fair and freshly coloured, with finely arched eyebrows, bright eyes, pink ears and red lips. He carried himself boldly, with a bearing that was neither Spanish nor Jesuit. On his orders Candide and Cacambo were given back their arms and horses. Cacambo had oats brought for the animals, and tethered them close to the arbour, where he kept his eye on them for fear of some trickery.

Candide kissed the hem of the Commandant's robe, and they sat down to table. 'So you are a German?' said the Jesuit, in that language.

'Yes, Reverend Father.' The two men suddenly looked at each other with amazement and emotion.

'From what part of Germany do you come?'

'From Westphalia. I was born in the castle of Thunder-ten-Tronckh.'

'Oh, heavens, can it be?'

'What a miracle!'

'Can it be you?'

'It is not possible!' They both reeled backwards, and then embraced, weeping.

'So you, Reverend Father, are the fair Cunégonde's brother! But I thought you were slain by the Bulgarians. But how come you, the Baron's son, to be a Jesuit in Paraguay? What a strange world! Ah, Pangloss, what joy this would have given you, if you had not been hanged!'

The negro and Paraguayan slaves, who were serving wine in crystal goblets, withdrew on the commandant's order.

With exclamations of praise to God and St. Ignatius, he clasped Candide in his arms. Their faces were wet with tears.

'You will be still more overcome', said Candide, 'when I tell you that Mistress Cunégonde, your sister, has not been disembowelled, as you supposed, but is in perfect health.'

'Where is she?'

'Not far from here, at the house of the Governor of Buenos Aires. I came here to fight you.'

Throughout a long conversation, they continued to marvel more and more, talking volubly and hanging on each other's words, with shining eyes. In German fashion, they lingered long at table, waiting for the Reverend Father Provincial. Meanwhile the commandant told his story:

CHAPTER XV

THE JESUIT BARON

'I SHALL never forget the dreadful day when I saw my father and mother slain, and my sister ravished. When the Bulgarians went, my sister was nowhere to be found. The bodies of my parents and myself, with those of the servant maids and of three little boys, all of whose throats had been cut, were thrown upon a cart, to be buried in a Jesuit chapel that lies two leagues from the castle.

'A Jesuit sprinkled us with holy water. It was dreadfully salt, and a few drops of it went into my eyes. The Father saw my eyelids stir, put his hand on my heart and felt it beating. I was cared for, and in three weeks was completely recovered.

'As you will remember, my dear Candide, I was a very handsome lad. I became still more so, and the Reverend Father Croust, Superior of the House, took a great fancy to me. He gave me the novice's habit, and in a short time I was sent to Rome. Our Genera was recruiting young German Jesuits. The rulers of Paraguay admit as few Spanish Jesuits as possible; they prefer those of other nations, as being more easily governed. The Reverend Father General considered me a fit person to come and labour in this vineyard. I set out with a Pole and a Tyrolese, and on arrival was given a subdeaconship and a lieutenancy. I am now a priest and a colonel.

'We shall give a warm reception to the King of Spain's troops, I can assure you. They will be beaten first, and excommunicated afterwards. Providence has sent you hither to assist us.

'But is it really true that my sister Cunégonde is with the Governor of Buenos Aires?' Candide solemnly assured him that it was so, and again tears trickled down their cheeks. The baron repeatedly embraced Candide, calling him his brother and deliverer.

'Perhaps, dear Candide,' he said, 'we shall enter the city together as victors, and recover my sister.'

'That is all that I desire; for I intended to marry her, and still hope to do so.'

'What, insolent fellow! You would have the impudence to marry my sister, who has seventy-two quarterings! Really you have an assurance, even to speak to me of such an audacious design!'

Candide was thunderstruck. 'Reverend Father,' he said, 'what are all the quarterings in the world? I have delivered your sister from the clutches of a Jew and an Inquisitor. She is grateful to me, and wishes to marry me. Master Pangloss always told me that all men are equal. I shall marry her, depend upon it!'

'We shall see about that, villain!' said the Jesuit Baron von Thunder-ten-Tronckh, and struck Candide across the face with the flat of his sword. Candide also drew, and plunged his sword up to the hilt in the Jesuit's belly. Then, pulling it out reeking hot, he burst into tears. 'O God!' he said, 'I have killed my old master, my friend, my brother-in-law. I am the mildest man in the world, yet I have already killed three men—and two of them were priests.'

Cacambo, who was standing guard at the gate of the arbour, came to see what had happened. 'Nothing remains to us but to sell our lives dear', said his master. 'Someone is bound to enter the arbour soon. We must die sword in hand.' But Cacambo had been in many such scrapes before, and kept calm. In a few seconds he stripped the Baron of his Jesuit's habit, put it on Candide, gave him the dead man's three-cornered hat, and made him mount.

'Gallop, master!' he said. 'Everybody will take you for a Jesuit on a tour of inspection. We shall have passed the frontier before they even start after us.' He rode rapidly ahead, shouting in Spanish: 'Make way, make way for the Reverend Father Colonel!'

CHAPTER XVI

THE GIRLS AND THE MONKEYS

By the time the German Jesuit's death was known in the camp, Candide and his valet were beyond the barriers. Cacambo had providently filled his wallet with bread, chocolate, ham, fruit and a few bottles of wine.

They rode on into an unexplored and pathless region, until they came to a beautiful meadow cut across by streams. Here they set their horses to graze. Cacambo advised his master to eat, and did so himself. 'How can you desire me to eat ham,' said Candide, 'when I have killed his lordship's son, and am doomed never to see Cunégonde again? What will it avail me to drag out a wretched existence, far from her, in remorse and despair? And what will the *Journal de Trevoux*[1] say?' Nevertheless, he ate.

The sun was now setting. The wanderers heard some faint cries, which seemed to have been uttered by women. They could not make out if these were cries of grief or of joy; but they rose hastily to their feet, with the disquiet that is caused by any unexpected event in an unknown country.

The cries, they now perceived, came from two young women, who were running nimbly along the edge of the meadow, pursued by two monkeys, which were biting their buttocks. Candide had learnt musketry with the Bulgarians, and could hit a filbert in a hedge without touching a leaf. He picked up his double-barrelled Spanish musket and killed both monkeys. 'God be praised, my dear Cacambo,' he said, 'I have rescued these two poor creatures from a grave peril. If it was a sin to kill an Inquisitor and a Jesuit, I have atoned for it by saving two girls' lives. Perhaps they are young ladies of good family, and this adventure may be of great service to us in this country.'

He was suddenly silenced by the sight of the two girls, who were affectionately embracing the dead monkeys, weeping and lamenting. 'Really,' he said, 'I would never have expected so much Christian charity.'

'You have done a fine stroke there, master!' said Cacambo, 'You have killed these two ladies' lovers.'

'Their lovers! You are jesting, Cacambo.'

'My dear master, everything surprises you. Why do you think it strange that there should be a country where monkeys win ladies' favours? They are a fourth part men, as I am a fourth part Spaniard.'

'Indeed,' said Candide with a sigh, 'I remember my master Pangloss telling me that such freaks were common

---

[1] A celebrated literary review, edited by members of the Society of Jesus throughout the first half of the eighteenth century.

in former times, and that these conjunctions produced egipans, fauns and satyrs, which were actually seen by many of the ancients; but I took all these tales for fables.'

'Now you see that they were true—and you see how people behave if they have not received a certain education. But what I fear is that these ladies may do us some mischief.'

This prudent remark persuaded Candide to leave the meadow and plunge into a wood. He and Cacambo finished their supper, and then, cursing the Inquisitor, the Governor of Buenos Aires and the Baron, they went to sleep in the undergrowth.

When they awoke, they could not move. During the night the Oreillons—this was the name of the local tribe— had learnt of their presence from the two ladies, and had tied them up with ropes made of bark. They were now surrounded by about fifty naked Oreillons armed with bows and arrows, clubs and flint-headed axes. Some were bringing a large cauldron to the boil, whilst others prepared spits. 'A Jesuit, a Jesuit!' they shouted. 'We shall be revenged, and shall have a good meal. Let us eat the Jesuit, eat the Jesuit!'

'I told you, master,' said Cacambo, 'that those wenches would play a scurvy trick on us.'

'We are certainly about to be either boiled or roasted. Ah, what would Pangloss say to this example of the behaviour of natural man in his pure state? Everything is good, says he. That may be; but I confess that it is hard to have lost Mistress Cunégonde, and then to be impaled on a spit by the Oreillons.'

'Do not lose hope. I understand a little of the jargon of these people, and will speak to them.'

'Be sure you point out to them how inhuman it is to boil and roast one's fellow-men, and how much at variance with Christian teaching.'

43

'Gentlemen,' said Cacambo, 'you no doubt suppose that today you are going to eat a Jesuit. 'Tis very well: indeed, no manner of treating an enemy could be more appropriate. The law of nature teaches us: "Thou shalt kill thy neighbour"—and this teaching is followed all over the world. If we in Europe neglect our right also to eat him, it is because we have better fare. But you have not such resources as we; and certainly it is better to eat one's enemies than to abandon the fruits of victory to the ravens and carrion-crows.

'But, gentlemen, you would not wish to eat your friends. It is not a Jesuit whom you are planning to roast, but your defender, the enemy of your enemies. For myself, I was born in your country. This gentleman is my master, and so far from being a Jesuit, he has lately killed one, and is wearing the spoils taken from him. That is how you came to make your mistake.

'To confirm the truth of what I say, take his habit to the nearest barrier of the Jesuit kingdom, and inquire whether my master did not kill one of their officers. It will take you little time; and, if I have lied to you, you can always eat us later. But if I have told you the truth, you know too well the laws of society, humanity and justice not to show us clemency.'

The Oreillons thought this speech very reasonable. They deputed two of their leading men to go at once and learn the truth. These two performed their task intelligently, and soon returned with favourable news. The Oreillons unbound their captives, treated them with great courtesy, offering them women and refreshments, and led them to the frontier of their country, gaily shouting: 'He is no Jesuit, he is no Jesuit!'

'What men, what manners!' thought Candide. 'Had I not been so fortunate as to have run Cunégonde's brother through the body, I should inexorably have been eaten. But, after all, pure natural man has much to be said for him: these people showed me a thousand civilities, the moment they knew I was not a Jesuit.'

CHAPTER XVII

EL DORADO—1

'WELL,' said Cacambo to his master, when they were at the frontier of the Oreillons, 'as you see, this hemisphere is no better than the other. Take my advice, and let us return to Europe the shortest way.'

'But how, and whither? In my own country the Bulgarians and Abarians are laying all waste. If I return to Portugal, I shall be burnt. If we abide here, we are every moment in danger of being roasted on spits. But how can I bring myself to quit that part of the world which contains Mistress Cunégonde?'

'Let us make for Cayenne. We shall find Frenchmen there—they are everywhere—and they will be able to help us. Perhaps God will take pity on us.'

It was not easy to reach Cayenne. They knew more or less in which direction to travel, but the way was barred by mountains, rivers, precipices, brigands and savages. Their horses died of fatigue and their provisions ran out. For a month they lived on wild fruit.

At length they came to a stream bordered by coconut palms. The sight of these gave them new life and hope. Cacambo, who was as ready with advice as the old woman, said: 'We are exhausted, and can march no farther. I spy an empty canoe; let us fill it with coconuts, embark, and drift down with the current. A river always leads to some inhabited place. If we find nothing pleasant, at least we shall find something new.'

'Agreed. Let us place ourselves in the hands of Providence.'

For a few leagues they were wafted between banks that were sometimes flowery, sometimes barren, sometimes level, sometimes rugged. The river gradually widened, until it reached a point where it disappeared into a tunnel beneath huge, terrifying crags. They decided to risk entering the tunnel, although the river, which had narrowed at this point, carried them along with dreadful speed and noise.

Twenty-four hours later they again saw daylight; but just as they did so, their canoe was dashed to pieces on a reef. For a whole league they had to drag themselves from rock to rock. Then the ravine opened out upon an immense horizon, rimmed with inaccessible mountains.

The country appeared to be cultivated as much for beauty as for the production of crops. On the roads were many carriages, of lovely design and made of some glittering material, carrying men and women of remarkable good looks and drawn by big red sheep, which were faster than the best horses of Andalusia, Tetuan or Mequinez.

'Here is a country that beats Westphalia', said Candide. They struck up from the river bank towards the first village they saw. Some village children, dressed in tattered gold brocade, were playing quoits by the entrance. The two Europeans noticed with interest that the quoits were large round discs, yellow, red, and green, of remarkable brilliance. They were, in fact, lumps of gold, ruby and emerald. The travellers felt a strong desire to collect some of them: the smallest would have made the biggest ornament in the throne of the Great Mogul.

'These children must be the sons of the king of this country', said Cacambo. At this moment the village teacher came to call the children back to their lessons. 'There is the royal family's tutor', said Candide.

The urchins left their quoits, and a number of other toys

lying on the ground. Candide picked them up and respectfully handed them to the teacher, indicating by signs that their Royal Highnesses had forgotten their gold and jewels. The teacher smiled, threw the objects down, glanced at Candide in surprise and followed the children back to the school.

The travellers carefully collected the treasures. 'What a strange country!' said Candide. 'The royal children here must be very properly educated, since they are taught to despise gold and precious stones.'

They approached the first house in the village, which was built on the scale of a European palace. There was a crowd of people by the gate, and a greater number inside. Delightful music, and a savoury smell of cooking, came from the house. Cacambo went up to the gate, and heard the people talking Peruvian. This was his mother tongue—as was previously mentioned, he was born in Tucuman, and in his native village only Peruvian was spoken.

'I will be your interpreter', he told Candide. 'This is an inn, let us enter.'

Two waiters and two maids, all dressed in cloth of gold and wearing ribbons in their hair, invited them to sit down to the ordinary. Dinner consisted of four different soups, each garnished with two parrots, a boiled condor weighing two hundred pounds, two roasted monkeys of excellent flavour, three hundred humming-birds in one dish and six hundred fly-catchers in another, and a number of delicious ragoûts and tarts. The whole meal was served in dishes of a kind of rock-crystal. The servants passed around liquors of various kinds, extracted from the sugar-cane.

Most of the company were pedlars and waggoners. They all had excellent manners: they asked Cacambo a few circumspect questions, and answered his questions willingly and fully.

After dinner Candide and Cacambo deposited on the table two of the big gold pieces that they had picked up, thinking that these would amply pay for their meal. The landlord and landlady burst out laughing. 'We can see that you are strangers here, gentlemen', said the landlord. 'We are not accustomed to such, so you must pardon us for laughing when you offer to pay us with stones off the high-road. No doubt you are not supplied with coin of this realm; but you need none, to dine here. All inns established for the convenience of merchants are paid for by the government. You have dined ill here, because this is a poor village; but everywhere else you will be received fittingly.'

Cacambo translated the gist of all this to Candide, whose surprise and bewilderment were as great as his valet's. 'What sort of a country is this,' said Cacambo, 'cut off from all the rest of the world, where nothing happens as it does amongst us?'

'Probably this is the country where everything is good—for there must be such a country somewhere; and, whatever Pangloss may have said, I often perceived that by no means everything was good in Westphalia.'

CHAPTER XVIII

EL DORADO—2

CACAMBO kept plying the landlord with questions, until the latter remarked: 'I am a most ignorant man, and content to remain so. But we have here an old man, a former servant of the court, who is more learned, and also more communicative, than anyone else in the kingdom.' He led Cacambo—accompanied by Candide, who was content to play a secondary part, as his valet's companion—to the old man's house.

It was a very modest dwelling, the door being made only

of silver, and the wainscoting only of gold; but both were so elegantly wrought as to bear comparison with the most sumptuous. The ante-chamber was a plain affair of rubies and emeralds; but here, too, good taste atoned for extreme simplicity.

The old man seated his visitors on a sofa stuffed with humming-birds' feathers, had drinks brought to them in diamond goblets, and proceeded to satisfy their curiosity.

'I am one hundred and seventy-two years old,' he said, 'and my late father, who was equerry to the King, told me of the amazing revolutions that he had witnessed in Peru. The kingdom in which you find yourselves is the ancient country of the Incas, who very imprudently sallied from it to conquer another part of the world, and were themselves in the end destroyed by the Spaniards.

'Some of the royal princes were wiser than the others, and remained in their native country. With the people's consent they made a law that no inhabitant of our little kingdom should ever leave it. To this we owe the preservation of our innocence and happiness.

'The Spaniards had some confused knowledge of this country, which they called El Dorado; and an Englishman, a knight named Raleigh, actually came very near it about a hundred years ago. But the unscalable rocks and precipices by which we are surrounded have always hitherto sheltered us from the rapacity of the European nations, who have an unaccountable fondness for the pebbles and dirt of our land, for the sake of which they would kill us all to the last man.'

A long conversation followed, concerning the country's form of government, its customs, women, public spectacles and arts. Candide, with his taste for metaphysics, inquired through Cacambo if the country had a religion.

The old man reddened a little. 'Can you doubt it?' he said. 'Do you take us for ingrates?'

Cacambo respectfully asked what was the religion of El Dorado, and the old man grew redder. 'Can there be two religions, then? We have, so I suppose, the same religion as the rest of the world. We worship God from morning till night.'

'Do you worship a single God?' asked Cacambo, still acting as Candide's interpreter.

'Certainly. There are not two, three or four Gods. I must confess that the people of your world ask most singular questions.'

Candide, however, persisted with his interrogation. He asked in what manner people prayed in El Dorado.

'We do not pray at all. We have nothing to ask of God. He has given us all we want, and we unceasingly give Him thanks.'

Candide next inquired where could he find the priests of this religion. The old man smiled: 'My friends,' he said, 'we are all priests. The King and all the heads of families sing hymns of thanksgiving each morning, accompanied by five or six thousand musicians.'

'Then have you no monks among you, to teach, dispute, govern, intrigue, and burn people who disagree with them?'

'Do you take us for madmen? There is no disagreement among us; and I do not know what you mean by monks.'

Candide was delighted. 'This is very different from Westphalia,' he thought, 'and also from his lordship's castle. If friend Pangloss had ever seen El Dorado he would never have said that the castle of Thunder-ten-Tronckh was the finest thing on earth. There is nothing like seeing the world, that's certain.'

At the end of the conversation the old man put at the travellers' disposal a coach drawn by six sheep, with twelve of his servants, to conduct them to court. 'Excuse me,' he said, 'that my age deprives me of the honour of accompanying you. The King will receive you in a manner with which you will have no fault to find. If certain of the customs of the country do not please you, no doubt you will make allowances.'

The six sheep drew them at a great pace, and in less than four hours Candide and Cacambo arrived at the royal palace, which was on the outskirts of the capital. The portal was two hundred and twenty feet high and a hundred feet wide. It is impossible to describe the material of which it was made; it may be imagined, however, that it was far superior to the pebbles and sand which in Europe are called gold and jewels.

On leaving the coach, Candide and Cacambo were received by twenty beautiful maids-in-waiting, who conducted them to the baths and dressed them in garments made of the down of humming-birds. They were then led by high officials of both sexes to His Majesty's apartment. They passed between two rows of musicians, each numbering a thousand men, according to the local custom.

As they approached the presence chamber, Cacambo asked an official how they should salute His Majesty. Should they fall on their knees, or flat on their stomachs? Should they put their hands on their heads, or behind their backs? In short, what was the procedure?

'It is customary', said the official, 'to embrace the King, and to kiss him on both cheeks.' Candide and Cacambo did this, and were cordially welcomed by His Majesty, who invited them to sup with him.

In the meantime they were shown the city. The public buildings seemed almost to touch the clouds. The market places were adorned with thousands of columns. Fountains of clear water, rose-water and liquors drawn from the sugar-cane played incessantly in the squares, which were paved with jewels that gave off an odour like that of cloves and cinnamon.

Candide asked to see the courts of justice and the parliament. He learnt that there were no such things, and that there was no litigation in El Dorado. He asked if there were any prisons, and learnt that there were none. What surprised and pleased him still more was the Palace of the Sciences, where he saw a gallery two thousand yards long, filled with mathematical and scientific instruments.

In the course of the whole afternoon they saw perhaps a thousandth part of the city. They were then led back to the palace, where they sat down to table with His Majesty and several ladies. The dinner was excellent, and His Majesty a most entertaining host. Cacambo translated his jokes, which, as Candide noted with surprise, were witty even in translation.

They spent a month as the King's guests, and Candide began to get restive. 'I admit', he said to Cacambo, 'that the castle where I was born is nothing to this place. But, when all's said, Mistress Cunégonde is not here; and you, too, doubtless have some beloved one in Europe. If we remain here, we shall be only as the other inhabitants; whereas, if we return to our own world with but a dozen sheep laden with the pebbles of El Dorado, we shall be richer than all the kings of Europe, we shall have nothing to fear from the Inquisition, and we may easily recover Mistress Cunégonde.'

Cacambo agreed. The desire for freedom of movement, to cut a figure amongst their own people, and to tell their travellers' tales, induced these fortunate beings to forsake their good fortune. They asked His Majesty for leave to depart.

'You are acting foolishly', said the King. 'I know that my country is nothing very great. But when one is tolerably at ease in any place, he should remain there. I have, of course, no power to detain strangers: that would be an act of tyranny at variance both with our manner of life and with our code of law. All men are free—go when you will.

'But you will not find it easy. It is impossible to ascend the swift river by which you miraculously came, or to pass through the rocky tunnel. The mountains entirely surrounding my kingdom are ten thousand feet high, and as steep as walls. The passage from one side of them to the other is of more than ten leagues, and the descent on the far side is barred by precipices.

'However, since you are so set on leaving us, I will order the superintendents of machines to make one to help you on your journey. When you are beyond the crest, nobody can accompany you any farther; for my subjects have taken a vow never to pass beyond our frontier, and are too wise to break it. Anything else you ask, you shall have.'

'All we ask of Your Majesty', said Candide, 'is a few sheep laden with victuals, pebbles and the clay of your country.'

The King smiled: 'I cannot imagine what pleasure you Europeans find in our yellow clay. But take away as much as you will, and much good may it do you.'

On the King's orders, his engineers made a machine to hoist these two extraordinary men out of the kingdom. It took three thousand skilled engineers a fortnight to finish the work, which cost more than twenty million pounds sterling in the currency of the country. Candide and Cacambo were placed on the machine, together with two large red sheep saddled and bridled to carry them after they had crossed the mountains, twenty baggage sheep laden with victuals, thirty carrying gifts of rich native workmanship, and fifty laden with gold, diamonds and other jewels.

When they and their sheep had been ingeniously hoisted to the summit of the mountains, the engineers took leave of them. Candide was filled with the thought of presenting his sheep to Cunégonde. 'Now we have wherewithal to pay the Governor of Buenos Aires,' he said, 'if Mistress Cunégonde is to be had at any price whatsoever. Let us make for Cayenne, and take ship there. Then let us see what kingdom we shall purchase.'

CHAPTER XIX

THE DUTCH SHIPMASTER

THE first day's journey was pleasant, for the two travellers were heartened by the thought that they possessed more wealth than Asia, Europe and Africa put together. Deliciously day-dreaming, Candide carved Cunégonde's name on trees.

On the second day, two of their sheep were swallowed up in swamps, with their loads. Two more died of fatigue a few days later. Subsequently seven or eight starved to death in a desert, and some others fell down precipices. After a hundred days of travel they had only two sheep left.

'You see, my friend,' Candide remarked to Cacambo, 'how perishable are the riches of this world. Nothing lasts but virtue, and the bliss of again seeing Mistress Cunégonde.'

'No doubt', said Cacambo. 'But we have still two sheep left, with more treasure than ever the King of Spain will own; and yonder I see a city which I take to be Surinam, a colony of the Dutch. We are at the end of our troubles, and the beginning of our pleasures.'

Near the city they found a negro lying on the ground. He wore only a pair of blue linen breeches, and his left leg and right hand had been cut off. 'My God,' said Candide in Dutch, 'what dost thou here, friend, in this deplorable condition?'

'I am waiting for my master, Mynheer Vanderendur, the great merchant', said the negro.

'Was it he that used you thus?'

'Yes, sir; it is the custom here. They give us a pair of linen breeches twice a year, and that is all our covering. When we labour in the sugar-works, and the mill catches a finger, they cut off a hand. When we try to run away, they cut off a leg. I have suffered both these misfortunes. This is the price at which you eat sugar in Europe.

'But 'tis strange to think that, when my mother sold me for ten pattacoons on the Guinea coast, she said to me: "Dear child, bless our Fetishes and adore them always. They will make you live happily. You have the honour to be the slave of our lords the whites, and you are making the fortune of your father and mother." Alas, I know not whether I have made their fortune; but they have not made mine. Dogs, monkeys and parrots are a thousand times less wretched than the like of us. The Dutch Fetishes who converted me tell us every Sunday that all men, blacks and whites, are the children of Adam. I know nothing of genealogies; but, if what these preachers say be true, we are all first cousins—and you must allow that no one could treat relations more horribly.'

'Ah, Pangloss!' Candide exclaimed, 'you never guessed at such an abomination! This is the end. I must renounce your optimism.'

'Optimism,' said Cacambo, 'what is that?'

'It is the madness of asserting that everything is good, when it is evil.' Candide looked again at the negro, and burst into tears: thus, weeping, he entered Surinam.

They at once inquired if there were a vessel in the harbour which would put in to Buenos Aires. The person they spoke to happened to be a Spanish shipmaster, who offered them reasonable terms, and made an appointment with them at an inn. Candide and Cacambo went there to wait for him, taking with them their two sheep.

When they met, Candide, who always blurted out whatever was foremost in his mind, told the Spaniard all his adventures and disclosed his intention of carrying off Mistress Cunégonde.

'In that case, I would not dream of carrying you to Buenos Aires', said the shipmaster. 'I should be hanged, and so should you. The fair Cunégonde is the Governor's favourite mistress.'

Candide was aghast at this news, and wept for a long time. Then he took Cacambo aside. 'I'll tell you what you must do, my dear friend', he said. 'Each of us has in his pockets diamonds to the value of five or six millions. You are more clever than I. Go to Buenos Aires and bring off Mistress Cunégonde. If the Governor makes any difficulty, give him a million. If he holds out, give him two. You have not killed an Inquisitor, so they have nothing against you.

'For my part, I'll fit out another ship and go to Venice, where I will wait for you. Venice is a free country, where we shall have nothing to fear from Bulgarians or Abarians, Jews or Inquisitors.'

Cacambo thoroughly agreed with this proposal. He was unhappy at parting from a good master, who had become his close friend; but the pleasure of doing him a service outweighed the grief of leaving him. He set out the same day, having been reminded by Candide not to forget the old woman. Cacambo was a very good man.

Candide remained some time longer in Surinam, waiting for another captain to carry him and his two remaining sheep to Italy. He engaged servants, and bought all that he needed for a long voyage. At length the merchant Mynheer Vanderendur, who was master of a large vessel, offered his services.

'What will you take', said Candide, 'to carry me, my servants, my baggage and these two sheep directly to

Venice?' The shipmaster asked ten thousand piastres, and Candide immediately agreed.

'Ho, ho!' thought Vanderendur, 'this foreigner must be very rich.' A little while later, he came back and said that he could not sail for less than twenty thousand. 'Very well, you shall have them', said Candide.

'Zounds!' muttered the shipmaster. Coming back a second time, he raised his price to thirty thousand piastres. 'You shall have them', said Candide.

'Ho, ho!' again thought the Dutchman, 'thirty thousand piastres are nothing to this man. Those sheep must certainly be laden with an immense treasure. I'll ask no more at present, but make him first pay the thirty thousand, and then we shall see.'

Candide sold two small diamonds, the smaller of which was worth all the money that the shipmaster demanded, and paid him in advance. The two sheep were put on board, and Candide took a small boat to join the ship in the roads. The shipmaster seized his opportunity, hoisted his sails, and put to sea with a favourable wind.

Bewildered and stupefied, Candide soon lost sight of the ship. 'Alas,' he exclaimed, 'this is a trick worthy of the world to which I am returning.' Crushed with grief, he put back to the shore, having lost the wealth of twenty monarchs.

His next act was to visit the Dutch magistrate. Being somewhat agitated, he banged violently on the door, and in stating his case spoke a little louder than was necessary. The magistrate fined him ten thousand piastres for making so much noise: after which he listened patiently, promised to look into the matter as soon as the merchant returned, and charged another ten thousand piastres for the costs of the hearing.

This behaviour reduced Candide to utter desperation. He

57

had in his lifetime suffered far worse misfortunes than this; but the cool impudence of the magistrate, coming on top of the villainy of the shipmaster, inflamed his choler and plunged him in a black melancholy. The wickedness of mankind presented itself nakedly before him, and he became obsessed with gloomy thoughts.

Shortly afterwards he learnt that a French ship was about to sail for Bordeaux. As he had no more sheep laden with diamonds, he hired a cabin at a reasonable price. He also advertised in the town that he would pay passage, board, and two thousand piastres to any honest man who would accompany him on the voyage; a condition being, that this man must be the most unfortunate, and the most dissatisfied with his lot, in the whole province.

The crowd of candidates who presented themselves was larger than a whole fleet could carry. Seeking to narrow the field of choice, Candide selected about twenty men who seemed congenial, and invited them to dine with him at his inn. He stipulated that each of them should undertake to give a true account of his life; whilst Candide, for his part, promised to choose as his companion the man who should seem to him the most deserving of compassion, and the most justly dissatisfied with his lot. He also promised to give each of the others a small present.

The session lasted until four in the morning. Candide was reminded of what the old woman had said on the voyage to Buenos Aires, when she wagered that every single person on board the ship had suffered great misfortunes. As each story was told, he thought to himself: 'Pangloss would be hard put to it now to maintain his favourite thesis. For sure, if everything is good, it can only be in El Dorado, and nowhere else on earth.'

Candide finally decided in favour of a poor scholar who had worked for ten years for the book publishers of

Amsterdam—no employment, he reflected, could be more disgusting than this. This scholar (who was, as it happened, a very good sort of man) had been robbed by his wife, beaten by his son and forsaken by his daughter, who had eloped with a Portuguese. He had lost the small employment by which he lived, and was being persecuted by the clergy of Surinam, who thought that he was a Socinian.

It must be admitted that all the other candidates were at least as unfortunate as this one. Candide's real reason for choosing him was a hope that, being a well-read man, he would relieve the tedium of the voyage. The other candidates all thought that Candide was doing them an injustice; but he appeased them by giving each a thousand piastres.

CHAPTER XX

MARTIN THE MANICHÆAN

CANDIDE and the old scholar, whose name was Martin, had both of them seen and suffered so much that even if the ship had been sailing from Surinam to Japan, *via* the Cape of Good Hope, the subject of moral and physical evil could have kept them busy talking throughout the voyage.

Candide, however, had one great advantage over Martin: he still hoped to see Cunégonde again, whereas Martin had nothing to look forward to. Moreover, Candide had money and jewels. True, he had lost eighty red sheep laden with the world's greatest treasure, and he was still vexed by the roguery of the Dutch shipmaster: nevertheless, when he thought of what he still had in his pockets, or spoke of Cunégonde—and especially after a good dinner— he continued to incline towards the doctrines of Pangloss.

'Tell me, Mr. Martin,' he said, 'what is your opinion of the whole matter? What notion have you of moral and physical evil?'

'Sir, the clergy have accused me of being a Socinian. But the truth is, I am a Manichæan.'

'Surely you are jesting. There are no Manichæans left in these times.'

'There is myself. I cannot help it. I can hold no other belief.'

'The devil must be in you, then.'

'Perhaps he is. He interferes so much in the world's affairs, he might as well be in my body as everywhere else. I confess that, when I contemplate this globe, or rather globule, I believe that God has handed it over—excepting always El Dorado—to some malignant being.

'I have seen scarcely a city that did not wish the ruin of its neighbouring city; nor a family that did not wish to exterminate some other family. Everywhere the weak hate the powerful, before whom they crawl, and the powerful treat the weak like sheep, selling their wool and their carcases.

'A million regimented assassins scour Europe, earning their livelihoods by authorized murder and brigandage, because this is regarded as the most glorious of trades.

'Even in cities that seem to be at peace, where the arts flourish, men are eaten up with envy, cares and disquiets worse than the sufferings of a town under siege. Secret chagrins are even more bitter than public calamities.

'In short, I have seen and experienced so much that I am a Manichæan.'

'Yet there is some good in the world.'

'May be so, but it has never come to my notice.'

This discussion was interrupted by the sound of gunfire, which grew louder. Taking out their glasses, they saw two ships fighting, about three miles away. The wind carried both ships so near to the French vessel that those on board the latter had the pleasure of watching the engagement in comfort. It ended when one of the ships sent the other to the bottom with a low and accurately aimed broadside. Candide and Martin could plainly see a hundred men gesticulating and shrieking on the deck of the sinking ship. A moment later, all were swallowed up.

'Well,' said Martin, 'you see how men treat one another.'

'Tis true, there is something diabolical in this business.'

As Candide spoke, he saw a brilliant red object floating close to their ship. The longboat was hoisted out, to discover what it was. It was one of his sheep. Candide felt more joy at the recovery of this one animal than he had felt grief at losing eighty of them, all laden with the treasures of El Dorado.

The French captain told them that the victorious ship was a Spaniard, and the other a Dutch pirate. Its skipper was, in fact, the very man who had robbed Candide. The immense riches which the scoundrel had thus acquired were now sunk with him in the sea.

'You see', said Candide, 'that crime is sometimes punished. That rascal of a Dutch skipper has met the fate he deserved.'

'Yes, but why should the passengers on his ship also perish? God may have punished the rogue, but the devil drowned the rest.'

The French and Spanish ships continued their cruise, and Candide and Martin continued their discussions. They argued for a fortnight, at the end of which they were as far advanced as at the beginning. However, the main thing was that they conversed, and in the exchange of ideas found consolation for their griefs.

Candide frequently embraced his sheep. 'Since I have found thee again,' he said to it, 'I may well find Cunégonde also.'

CHAPTER XXI

THE NATURE OF MANKIND

'WERE you ever in France, Mr. Martin?' asked Candide. They were within sight of the coast.

'Yes, I have passed through several of her provinces. In some, the half of the inhabitants are mad; in others, they are too artful; in others, they are mostly rather simple and stupid; in still others, they affect to be witty. In all of them, however, the chief occupation is making love, the second is slander, and the third is talking nonsense.'

'But have you seen Paris, Mr. Martin?'

'Yes, I have been there. It contains all the kinds I have mentioned. It is a chaos, a throng, where everyone seeks for pleasure, and, as far as I could make out, scarcely anyone finds it.

'On my arrival there, I had all my money stolen by pickpockets at the fair of Saint Germain. I myself was arrested as a thief, and imprisoned for a week. Afterwards I worked as a publisher's proof-reader, to earn enough to return to Holland on foot. I came to know the whole pack of scribblers, caballers and religious jumping-jacks.[1] Some of the people are said to be very polite. I would like to believe it.'

'For my part,' said Candide, 'I have no wish to see France. As you may well imagine, after spending a month in El Dorado there is nothing else on earth that I wish to see—excepting Mistress Cunégonde. I am going to wait

[1] In French, 'la canaille convulsionnaire'. 'Convulsionnaires' was the name given in the reign of Louis XV to a group of Jansenists who on occasion would go into fits of religious ecstasy similar to those of the negro 'holy rollers' of modern times.

for her at Venice, and will pass through France on my way to Italy. Will you not go with me?'

'Gladly. I have heard that life in Venice is pleasant only for the rich, but that visitors who have plenty of money are very well received there. I have none, but you have; so I shall follow you whither you please.'

'While we are on the subject, do you believe that the earth was originally sea, as is stated in that great book that belongs to the captain?'

'I believe nothing of the sort, any more than I do all the other fancies that have been foisted upon us through the centuries.'

'But to what end, think you, was the world formed?'

'To turn our brains.'

'Were you not astonished by that story I told you, of the two girls in the country of the Oreillons, who had monkeys for lovers?'

'Not in the least. I see nothing strange in such an infatuation. I have seen so many extraordinary things that now nothing is extraordinary to me.'

'Do you think that men always slaughtered one another, as they do nowadays? Were there always liars, cheats, traitors, brigands, weaklings, deceivers, cowards, enviers, gluttons, drunkards, misers, sycophants, butchers, slanderers, debauchees, fanatics, hypocrites and fools?'

'Do you think that hawks have always devoured pigeons at every opportunity?'

'Doubtless.'

'Well, then, if hawks have always been the same, why should men have been altered?'

'Ah, but there is a great difference, for Free Will . . .'

They were still arguing when they arrived at Bordeaux.

CHAPTER XXII

A RICH STRANGER IN PARIS

CANDIDE stayed in Bordeaux only long enough to sell a few of the pebbles of El Dorado, and to procure a good chaise with room for two people. He now found the philosopher Martin's company indispensable. He was distressed, however, at having to part with his sheep, which he gave to the Bordeaux Academy of the Sciences. The Academy proposed as the theme for its yearly prize competition an investigation into the reason for the redness of the sheep's wool. The prize was won by a scholar from the north, who demonstrated by $\dfrac{A + B - C}{Z}$ that the sheep must of necessity be red, and furthermore that it would die of the rot.

It struck Candide that all the travellers whom he met at inns along the road told him that they were going to Paris. This general eagerness to go there at length made him wish to see the city, which was not much out of the way to Venice.

He entered by the Faubourg St. Marceau, which was like one of the worst villages in Westphalia. On putting up at an inn, he was overtaken by a slight illness, caused by fatigue. Since he wore a huge diamond on one of his fingers, and had in his carriage a weighty strong-box, he was attended by two physicians, whom he had not asked for, by a number of close friends who were always by his bedside, and by two devoted females, who kept ordering cups of broth for him.

'I, too, have been ill in Paris,' said Martin, 'but I was

very poor, and had no friends, nurses or physicians. I recovered.'

As a result of purgings and bleedings, Candide's illness became serious. A priest of the parish came and offered to sell him a note of exchange, payable to the bearer in the other world.[1] Candide refused the transaction, although the two females assured him that it was the latest fashion. Candide told them that he was not a man of fashion, and Martin offered to throw the priest out of the window. The priest swore that Candide would not receive burial, and Martin swore that it was he who would bury the priest, if he continued to plague them. After a heated argument, Martin took the priest by the shoulders and turned him out of the room: this caused a great scandal, and information was laid against Candide with the authorities.

Candide recovered. During his convalescence a number of his attentive companions regularly came and dined with him. They played cards, for high stakes. Candide was surprised to find that he never held any aces: this did not surprise Martin.

Amongst Candide's visitors was a little abbé from Perigord, one of those obsequious, quick-witted, obliging, impudent, fawning, useful creatures who lie in wait for passing strangers, tell them the scandal of the town, and offer them pleasures at various prices. This abbé took Candide and Martin to the *Comédie*, where a new tragedy was being performed.

Candide's seat was next to a party of wits; but this did not prevent him from weeping at some moving and beautifully acted scenes. During an interval, one of the talkative bores who had been sitting near by remarked to him: 'You

[1] An allusion to the '*billets de confession*', which in Voltaire's time Catholic priests customarily demanded, before they would give the last sacrament.

should not have wept. That actress is wretched, and the actor who plays with her is even worse. The piece is worse than the actors. The author does not know a word of Arabic, yet he has laid his scene in Arabia. What is more, the fellow does not believe in innate ideas. Tomorrow I will bring you a score of pamphlets that have been written against him.'

Afterwards Candide asked the abbé how many theatrical pieces there were in France.

'Five or six thousand.'

''Tis a great number. How many of them are good?'

'Fifteen or sixteen.'

''Tis a great number.'

Candide was greatly taken with an actress who was one of the audience. She had made her name, so the abbé told him, by playing Queen Elizabeth in a rather dull tragedy that is still sometimes performed. 'I like that actress', said Candide. 'She has a deceiving resemblance to Mistress Cunégonde. I should be very glad to pay my respects to her.'

The abbé offered to introduce him to the actress at her house. Candide, having been brought up in Germany, wanted to know what was the etiquette, and how a stage Queen of England was treated in France.

'That depends on the circumstances', said the abbé. 'In a country town we take them to a tavern. Here in Paris they are treated with great respect while they are beautiful, and are thrown on a dunghill when they die.'

'A queen thrown on a dunghill!'

'Yes, the abbé is right', said Martin. 'I was in Paris when Mlle. Monime made her exit, as you may say, out of this world into another. She was refused what they call here "honours of sepulture", that is to say, she was denied the privilege of rotting in a mean churchyard with all the beggars of the parish. She was buried all by herself, at the corner of the Rue de Bourgogne; which must have shocked her extremely, as she had very exalted ideas.'

'That was far from polite', said Candide.

'What do you expect? These people are like that. Imagine to yourself all possible contradictions and inconsistencies: you will find them all in the government, the courts of justice, the churches and the public spectacles of this odd nation.'

'Is it true that Parisians are always laughing?'

'Yes,' said the abbé, 'but only in anger. They complain of everything with loud bursts of laughter. Even when themselves behaving in the most abominable manner, they laugh.'

'Who was that filthy great lout who spoke so ill of the piece that moved me so much, and of the players who gave me so much pleasure?'

'A good-for-nothing who gets his livelihood by abusing each book and play that appears. He hates everything successful as eunuchs hate great lovers. He is one of those literary vipers who feed on dirt and venom—a pamphleteer.'

'And what is that?'

'A hack journalist, a Fréron.'[1]

As they spoke, Candide, Martin and the abbé were standing on the main staircase of the theatre, watching the audience depart. 'Although my one wish is to see Mistress Cunégonde again,' said Candide, 'yet I should like to sup with Mlle. Clairon'—this was the name of the actress already mentioned—'for I much admired her.'

The abbé did not, in fact, dare to approach Mlle. Clairon, who was fastidious about the company she kept. 'She is engaged this evening,' he said, 'but I will do myself the honour to lead you to the house of a lady of quality, where

[1] Editor of the *Année littéraire*, and a bitter enemy of Voltaire.

67

you will come to know as much of Paris as if you had lived here for forty years.'

Candide, who was always eager for new experiences, agreed to visit the lady, who lived in the depths of the Faubourg St.-Honoré. The company was playing faro: a dozen gloomy punters held in front of them hands of cards—gloomy and preposterous registers of their misfortunes. There was a deep hush in the room; the punters were pale and the banker was tense.

The lady of the house sat by the banker and kept a lynx-like watch on the bidding, which consisted of mutters of 'double' or 'raise it seven times'. When one of the gamblers bent the corner of a card, she made him straighten it out. Her manner in so doing was strict, but polite: she showed no anger, so as not to frighten away her customers.

The name this lady went by was the Marquise de Parolignac. Her fifteen-year-old daughter was one of the punters, and made signs to her mother whenever one of the unfortunate gamesters tried to soften the rigours of chance by cheating.

When the abbé, Candide and Martin came in, nobody got up, greeted them or looked their way. 'My Lady Baroness of Thunder-ten-Tronckh would have behaved more civilly', thought Candide. The abbé whispered something to the marquise, who half raised herself from her chair and gave Candide a gracious smile and Martin a distant nod. She ordered a chair and a pack of cards to be fetched for Candide, who proceeded to lose fifty thousand francs in a few deals. After this the company had supper. Everyone marvelled at the calmness with which Candide bore his losses, and the lacqueys whispered that he must be an English milord.

The supper, like most suppers in Paris, opened in silence, which was followed first by a confused babble and then by the repetition of a number of jokes, mostly rather insipid, some inaccurate gossip, some pointless discussions, a little politics, and a great deal of scandal. There was even some talk about books. 'Has anyone read the new romance by the Doctor of Divinity, the Sieur Gauchat?'[1] the abbé asked the company.

'Yes,' replied one of the guests, 'but I had not the patience to go through with it. The town is pestered with a swarm of impertinent productions, but this of Dr. Gauchat's outdoes them all. Indeed, I am so cursedly tired of reading so much vile stuff that I have taken refuge in faro.'

'But what say you to Archdeacon Trublet's *Miscellany*?'[2]

'What a tedious creature!' said Mme. de Parolignac. 'What pains he is at to tell you what everybody knows already, and how he labours some point that is scarcely worth making! How clumsily he picks the brains of others—for he has none of his own—and how he mangles what he has pilfered! The man makes me sick: but he shall do so no longer—a few pages of the archdeacon are quite enough.'

One of the guests, who happened to be a man of learning and taste, agreed with the marquise. The conversation turned to plays, and the marquise asked why was it that so many utterly unreadable plays were still being performed. The man of taste explained that a piece of almost no merit may nevertheless have some interesting quality. It was not sufficient, he commented, for the author merely to throw together two or three of those situations which, though found in every romance, never lose their fascination for the public. A great work must be novel without being far-fetched; frequently sublime, but always natural. The author must know the human heart, and how to make it speak; he

[1] Author of a work entitled *Lettres sur quelques écrits de ce temps*.

[2] His principal work, *Essais de littérature et de morale*, was published in 1736.

must be a poet, without letting any of his characters speak like poets; and he must be a master of his language, using it purely and harmoniously and not letting the rhyme interfere with the sense.

'Whoever fails to observe any one of these conditions,' he concluded, 'though he may gain public applause with one or two plays, will never be reckoned in the number of good authors. There are very few good plays. Some of those that are produced are idylls cast in the form of dialogue, frequently well written and in good verse. Others are political tracts, which send one to sleep, or amplifications of the obvious, which are merely repellent. Others again are the fancies of a madman, composed in an uncouth style, with lapses into inconsequence, long apostrophes to the deities—inserted, doubtless, because the author does not know how to address his fellow-men—false maxims and stuffed-up commonplaces.'

Candide had listened with admiring attention. He now leant over to the marquise—she had arranged that he should be seated next to her—and asked in a whisper who this excellent talker might be.

'He is a man of letters', said the marquise. 'He does not play, but the abbé sometimes brings him to sup with me. He is a great judge of plays and books. He has himself written a play that was hissed off the stage, and a book that has never been seen outside his publisher's shop—except for one copy that he sent to me with a dedicatory inscription.'

'A truly great man,' said Candide, 'a second Pangloss!' Then, addressing the gentleman himself: 'Sir,' he said, 'I take it that you are of opinion that everything is for the best both in the physical and in the moral world, and that every-thing must be as it is?'

'I, sir! I think no such thing. I consider that everything in this world is awry; that no one knows his rank, his office, nor what he does nor what he should do; and that, except at supper, which is a fairly cheerful function and tends to produce concord, our time is spent on idle quarrels: Jansenists against Molinists, parliament against church, country against country, financiers against the people, women against their husbands, relations against relations. 'Tis a perpetual battlefield.'

'I have seen worse things than those you mention', said Candide. 'Yet a learned man, who has since had the misfortune to be hanged, taught me that everything was marvellously well, and that these evils are mere shadows in a beautiful picture.'

'Your gallows-bird was laughing at you', said Martin. 'These shadows, as you call them, are horrible blemishes.'

''Tis not men who make these blemishes; they cannot act otherwise than as they do.'

'Then it is not their fault.'

Most of the gamesters did not understand a word of all this, and were busy drinking. Martin continued the discussion with the man of letters, whilst Candide told the lady of the house some of his adventures.

After supper the marquise took Candide to her boudoir, where she sat him on a sofa. 'Well,' she said, 'are you still so violently fond of Mistress Cunégonde von Thunderten-Tronckh?'

'Yes, madam.'

The marquise smiled affectionately. 'You answer like a young Westphalian. A Frenchman would have said: "It is true that I loved Mistress Cunégonde. But since I have seen you, I fear that I love her no longer."'

'Alas, madam, I will make what answer you please.'

'You fell in love with her, I am told, when you picked up her handkerchief. You shall pick up my garter.'

'Most willingly, madam.' Candide did so.

'But now you must tie it on again.' Candide did this too.

'Look ye, young man, you are a stranger here. I make some of my Parisian lovers languish for me a whole fortnight; but I surrender to you the first night, because it is a patriotic obligation to show hospitality to a young man from Westphalia.'

Whilst speaking, the beauty noticed that the young foreigner was wearing two enormous diamonds. She praised them with such unaffected enthusiasm that they were soon transferred from Candide's fingers to hers.

As he went home with Martin and the abbé, Candide felt some remorse at having been unfaithful to Cunégonde. The abbé, too, was dissatisfied. He had received only a small share of the fifty thousand francs that Candide had lost at play—not to speak of the two diamonds—and he was planning how to turn his acquaintance with Candide to the greatest possible profit.

He began talking about Cunégonde, and Candide remarked that when he saw her again, he would humbly ask her pardon for his unfaithfulness. The abbé listened with courteous attention. He seemed to take a keen interest in everything that Candide said, did, or planned to do.

'And so, sir, you have an engagement at Venice?'

'Yes, Monsieur l'Abbé. I absolutely must find Mistress Cunégonde.' Carried away by the pleasure of talking of his beloved, Candide related, as he so often did, some of his adventures with that illustrious Westphalian damsel.

'I suppose', said the abbé, 'that Mistress Cunégonde has a great deal of wit, and writes charming letters?'

'Indeed, I have never received any from her. For you must remember that, having been driven out of the castle for my love of her, I could not write to her, and soon afterwards I learnt that she was dead. I then found her and lost her again, and now I have sent a messenger to her, near two thousand leagues from hence, and am waiting here for the answer.'

The abbé listened attentively, and seemed pensive. Soon afterwards he cordially embraced Candide and Martin, and left them.

Next morning Candide received the following letter:

'My dearest Lover, for the last week I have been in this city, confined by illness. I have learnt that you are here, and should fly to your arms, were I able to stir. I learnt of your arrival when I was at Bordeaux, where I have left the faithful Cacambo and the old woman. They will soon follow me. The Governor of Buenos Aires has taken everything from me but your heart. Come to me: your presence will either give me new life, or kill me with pleasure.'

Torn between joy at this charming and unexpected letter and grief at the news of Cunégonde's illness, Candide took his gold and diamonds and found a guide to lead Martin and himself to the hotel where she was lodging. When he entered her room, he trembled, his heart beat violently, and his voice quavered. He started to draw back the bed-curtains, and called for a light.

'Ah, beware of doing that, sir!' said the chambermaid. 'Mistress cannot bear the light.' She quickly pulled the curtains closed again.

'Dearest Cunégonde,' sobbed Candide, 'how are you faring? If you cannot see me, speak to me, at least.'

'She cannot speak', said the maid.

The lady put a plump hand outside the curtains. Candide wetted it with his tears, and then filled it with diamonds. He also laid a purse of gold on the chair by the bedside.

An officer entered the room, followed by the abbé and a squad of men. 'Are these the suspected foreigners?' he asked, and gave orders that they should be arrested and taken off to prison.

'Travellers are not treated in this manner in El Dorado', said Candide.

'I am more a Manichæan than ever', said Martin.

'But pray, officer, where are you going to carry us?'

'To a dungeon.'

Martin collected his wits and realized that the pretended Cunégonde, the abbé and the officer were all frauds, and that the officer could easily be got rid of. He enlightened Candide, and the latter, in his impatience to see the true Cunégonde, immediately offered the officer a bribe of three small diamonds, worth about three thousand pistoles each.

'Ah, sir,' said the man with the ivory tipstaff, 'had you committed ever so many crimes, you would still be the best man living. Three diamonds, worth several thousand pistoles, I'll be bound! Why, sir, so far from carrying you to jail, I would give my life for you.

'There are orders for the arrest of all foreigners, but leave it to me. I have a brother at Dieppe, in Normandy. I will conduct you thither, and if you have a diamond for him, he will take as much care of you as I myself should.'

'But why are they arresting foreigners?'

The abbé broke into the conversation: 'A poor devil of an Atrebatian listened to some foolish stories, which excited him to parricide.[1] It was a crime different from that of May 1610,[2] but similar to that of December 1594,[3] and, indeed, to many other crimes committed in various months and years by other poor devils who have listened to foolish stories.'

The officer explained what the abbé was talking about. 'The monsters!' Candide exclaimed. 'To think that such

---

[1] There was an attempted assassination of Louis XV on 5 January 1757.

[2] The assassination of Henri IV.

[3] An attempted assassination of Henri IV.

horrid deeds should be committed among a people that is always singing and dancing. How can I most quickly escape from this country, where monkeys give offence to tigers? For God's sake, officer, conduct me to Venice, where I am to wait for Mistress Cunégonde.'

'I cannot conduct you farther than the coast of Normandy', said the officer. He ordered Candide's and Martin's irons to be struck off, told his men that a mistake had been made, and dismissed them. He then brought Candide and Martin to Dieppe, where he left them to the care of his brother.

There was a small Dutch ship in the roads, and the officer's brother, whose devoted loyalty had been purchased for three more diamonds, put Candide and Martin aboard it. The ship was about to sail for Portsmouth, in England. This was not on the direct route to Venice, but Candide did not care. He felt that he had escaped from hell, and reckoned on resuming his journey to Venice at the first opportunity.

CHAPTER XXIII

'TO ENCOURAGE THE OTHERS'

'AH, Pangloss, Pangloss—ah, Martin, Martin—ah, dearest Cunégonde—what sort of a world is this?' So sighed Candide, aboard the Dutch vessel.

'Something utterly mad and abominable', said Martin.

'You know England. Are they as mad there as in France?'

'It is another kind of madness. As you know, these two nations are at war for the sake of a few acres of snow up towards Canada, and are spending on this fine war of theirs more than all Canada is worth. To say exactly whether there are more people fit for strait-waistcoats in the one country than in the other, exceeds the limits of my imperfect capacity. All I know is that, in general, the people we are going to visit are of an atrabilious disposition.'

At Portsmouth the shore was crowded with people eagerly watching a big man[1] who was kneeling on the deck of a man-of-war, with a bandage over his eyes. In front of him stood four soldiers, each of whom phlegmatically fired three bullets into the big man's skull. The crowd then dispersed, with an air of satisfaction.

'What is all this?' said Candide. 'What demon has the mastery of the world?' He inquired who the big man was. 'An admiral', he was told.

'And why was this admiral killed?'

'Because he did not kill enough men himself. He fought an engagement with a French admiral, and it is thought that he did not sufficiently close with him.'

'But surely, then, the French admiral was as far from him as he was from the other?'

'That is undeniable. But in this country it is found requisite now and then to kill an admiral, in order to encourage the others.'

Candide was so shocked that he would not set foot on shore. He struck a bargain with the Dutch skipper—wondering whether the latter would rob him, like the Dutch skipper at Surinam—for a direct passage to Venice.

The ship was ready to sail in two days. They sailed along the coast of France and passed within sight of Lisbon, at which Candide shuddered. They passed through the straits into the Mediterranean, and arrived at Venice. 'God be praised!' said Candide, embracing Martin. 'Here I shall see Cunégonde again. I trust Cacambo as I trust myself. Everything is good, as good as could possibly be.'

[1] Admiral Byng, who was executed on 14 March 1757.

CHAPTER XXIV

PAQUETTE AND FRIAR GIROFLÉE

IN Venice Candide looked for Cacambo at every inn and coffee-house, and among all the ladies of pleasure, but could not find him. He sent every day to inquire what ships had come in: still no news of Cacambo.

'What!' he said to Martin. 'Have I had time to travel from Surinam to Bordeaux, thence to Paris, to Dieppe, to Portsmouth, to sail along the coasts of Portugal and Spain and up the Mediterranean, to spend some months in Venice—and still Cunégonde is not arrived? All that I have found in her place has been a female trickster. Cunégonde is certainly dead, and I have nothing to do but to follow her.

'Alas, how much better it would have been to remain in the paradise of El Dorado, than to have returned to this cursed Europe! You are in the right, my dear Martin: all is misery and deceit in this wicked world.'

He fell into a black melancholy, and took no part in the *opera alla moda*, or in any other of the carnival festivities. Not one lady paid the least attention to him.

'Upon my word,' said Martin, 'you are very simple to imagine that a mestizo valet, with five or six millions in his pockets, would go to the end of the world in search of your mistress and bring her to you at Venice. If he finds her, he will keep her for himself. If he does not find her, he will take another. I advise you to forget your valet Cacambo, and your mistress, too.'

Martin was no comfort. Candide's melancholy grew, whilst Martin continued to demonstrate to him that there was very little virtue or happiness on earth—except possibly in El Dorado, where nobody could go.

One day Candide saw on the Piazza di San Marco a young Theatine friar, with a girl under his arm. The friar was clear complexioned, plump, bright-eyed and vigorous, with an assured manner and a bold and spirited mien and bearing. The girl, who was very pretty, was singing. Now and then she glanced lovingly at her Theatine, and pinched his chubby cheeks.

'You will allow', said Candide to Martin, 'that there, at least, are two happy people. Everywhere, hitherto—except in El Dorado—I have met only unfortunates. But as to this couple, I wager they are most happy creatures.'

'I wager they are not.'

'Well, we have only to ask them to dine with us, and you will see whether I am mistaken.'

Candide thereupon accosted the couple, and with a bow invited them to come to his inn and dine on macaroni, Lombard partridges and caviare, with Montepulciano, Lachryma Christi and Cyprian and Samian wines.

The Theatine accepted the invitation. The girl blushed and followed the friar unwillingly, repeatedly staring at Candide with an air of surprise and embarrassment, her eyes full of tears. When they reached the inn, the friar remained downstairs for a drink before dinner, whilst the others went to Candide's apartment. Here the girl said to him: 'How, Master Candide, do you not recognise Paquette?'

Candide had not hitherto looked at her closely, since he cared for no woman but Cunégonde. 'Ah, my poor child!' he now exclaimed, 'is it you? And was it you who reduced Dr. Pangloss to that fine condition in which I saw him?'

'Alas, yes, sir, it is I, indeed, and I see that you know everything. I have learnt of the dreadful misfortunes that befel the whole household of her ladyship the Baroness and Mistress Cunégonde. I vow to you that my own lot has been scarcely less pitiful.

'I was a good girl when you saw me last. I was seduced by a Franciscan friar, who was my confessor: the consequences proved terrible. I was obliged to leave the castle, only a little while after the Baron kicked you out. If a famous surgeon had not taken compassion on me, I had been a dead woman. Out of gratitude, I lived with him for some time as his mistress. His wife, who was ragingly jealous, beat me unmercifully every day. She was a fury! The doctor was the ugliest man alive, and surely I was the unhappiest of all creatures, to be continually beaten for a man whom I did not love.

'You know, sir, how dangerous it is for a cross-grained woman to be married to a doctor. Incensed at his wife's behaviour, he took his opportunity one day when she had a slight cold, and gave her a medicine so efficacious that she died within two hours, in frightful convulsions.

'Her relations brought a criminal action against the doctor, who fled. I was put in jail. My innocence would not have saved me, had I not been tolerably handsome. The judge set me free, on condition that he should succeed the doctor. But I was soon supplanted by a rival, turned off without a farthing, and obliged to take to the abominable trade which you men think so pleasing, but which to us is nothing but a bottomless pit of misery.

'I came to exercise the profession at Venice. Ah, sir, did you but know what it is to be obliged to lie with every fellow—with old tradesmen, councillors, monks, gondoliers, abbés; to be exposed to all their insults and outrages; to be often reduced to borrowing a petticoat, only that it may be lifted by some disgusting man; to be robbed by one man of what one has earned from another; to have to pay bribes to officers of justice; and to have no other prospect than a hideous old age, ending in a hospital or on a dunghill: did you but know all this, you would conclude that I am one of the most unhappy creatures alive.'

'You see,' said Martin, 'I have won half of my wager already.'

'But you seemed so gay and content when I met you', Candide said to Paquette. 'You sang, you caressed the Theatine with an air of such genuine fondness, that I thought you to be as happy as—so it now appears—you are in truth wretched.'

'Ah, sir, that is one of the miseries of the trade. Yesterday I was beaten and robbed by an officer: and today I must seem merry to please a monk.'

Candide had heard enough; he admitted that Martin had won his wager—at least, as far as Paquette was concerned. They went to join the friar for dinner.

The meal was a pleasant one, and towards the end they were talking freely. 'Father,' said Candide, 'you seem a most enviable man. Your face glows with health and happiness, you have a pretty wench to divert you, and you seem very content to be a friar.'

'Faith, sir,' said Friar Giroflée, 'I could wish all Theatines at the bottom of the sea. I have been tempted a thousand times to set fire to the monastery and turn Turk.

'My parents obliged me, at the age of fifteen, to put on this detestable habit, so that they might leave a greater inheritance to an accursed elder brother, whom God confound!

'Our monastery is full of jealousy, discord and fury. I get a little money by preaching a few paltry sermons: the Prior robs me of the half of it, but the remainder pays for wenches. Yet, when I return to the monastery at night, I am ready to dash my head against the walls of the dormitory: and all the rest of the brotherhood are in like case.'

'Well,' said Martin, 'I think I have now won the wager entirely.'

Candide gave two thousand piastres to Paquette and a thousand to the friar. 'My answer is,' he said, 'that now, with this money, they will be happy.'

'I don't believe it. Perhaps these piastres will make them more wretched still.'

'Be that as it may, one thing comforts me. I see that one often meets people whom one had never expected to meet again. I have found my red sheep, and Paquette. It may well be that I shall also find Cunégonde.'

'Indeed, I wish that one day she may bring you happiness: but I much doubt it.'

'You are very harsh.'

'I have seen the world.'

'But observe these gondoliers. Are they not always singing?'

'You do not see them at home with their wives and brats. The Doge has his griefs—gondoliers have theirs. It is true that, in the main, a gondolier's lot is preferable to that of a doge: but the difference is so trifling that it is not worth the trouble of inquiring into.'

'There is talk of a certain Senator Pococurante, who lives in that fine house on the Brenta, and is hospitable to foreigners. He is said to be a man who has never known grief.'

'I should be glad to meet so extraordinary a being.'

Candide thereupon sent a message to Senator Pococurante, asking for permission to visit him next day.

CHAPTER XXV

SENATOR POCOCURANTE

CANDIDE and Martin took a gondola to Senator Pococurante's palace on the Brenta. Its gardens were extensive and adorned with fine marble statues, and the palace itself was of great beauty. The master of the house, a man of about sixty, and very rich, received the two sightseers civilly, but without much ceremony. Candide was disconcerted by this, but Martin was rather pleased.

Two pretty girls in neat dresses brought chocolate, which they stirred into a creamy froth. Candide remarked on their good looks and smart service.

'They are good enough creatures', said the senator. 'I make them lie with me sometimes, for I am heartily tired of the city ladies, their coquetry, their jealousy, their quarrels, their humours, their meannesses, their pride and their follies. I am tired of making sonnets, or of paying for sonnets to be made, in their honour.

'But now, after all, these girls begin to tax my patience.'

After breakfast they walked along a large gallery. Candide admired the pictures. Pausing by the first two they came to, he asked who had painted them. 'They are by Raphael', said the senator. 'I bought them, at a great price, seven years ago, purely from vanity, as they are said to be the finest pieces in Italy. They do not please me: the colours are gloomy, the figures do not come out enough, they want relief, and the draperies do not at all resemble any true stuff. In short, whatever may be said of them, they are not, in my opinion, a true representation of nature. I shall never like a picture, unless it makes me believe that I am beholding Nature herself: and there are no such pictures. I have many, but I no longer look at them.'

Before dinner Pococurante ordered music. Candide thought it delightful. 'This noise', said Pococurante, 'may entertain one for half an hour, but if it lasts longer it becomes tiresome to everybody, although no one dares to own it. Music in these days is no more than the art of performing the difficult; and that which is merely difficult, and nothing else, cannot please for long.

'I believe I might take more pleasure in opera, if they had

not found a way to turn it into a repulsive monstrosity. These wretched tragedies set to music—see them who will: where the scenes are contrived for no other purpose than to introduce, most incongruously, two or three songs designed to give some actress an opportunity of showing the powers of her gullet. Let who will, or can, swoon with pleasure to see a eunuch trilling and strutting his way through the part of Cæsar or Cato. For my part, I have long since forsaken these paltry spectacles, which constitute the glory of our modern Italy—and for which monarchs pay so dear.'

Candide argued against these sentiments, but only a little and with discretion. Martin was in full agreement with them.

After an excellent dinner, they repaired to the library, where Candide noticed a magnificently bound Homer. He complimented the senator on the possession of this treasure. 'This book', he said, 'was once the delight of the great Pangloss, the best philosopher in Germany.'

'It is no delight to me', said Pococurante. 'At one time I was made to believe that I took pleasure in reading it. But the continual repetition of battles, which are all alike— those gods, who are always busy achieving nothing—that Helen, who is the cause of the war, yet scarcely plays a part in the whole performance—that interminable and ineffectual siege—I have found them all insufferably tedious. I have several times asked well-read men if they were as much wearied by the work as I was. All the honest ones confessed that they fell asleep while reading it, but had to have it in their libraries, like some rusty old medal that has no commercial value.'

'But Your Excellency surely does not hold the same opinion of Virgil?' asked Candide.

'I grant that the second, fourth and sixth books of his *Æneid* are excellent. But his pious Æneas, strong Cloanthus, faithful Achates, little Ascanius, and that imbecile King

Latinus and that vulgar Amata—nothing could be more flat or disagreeable. I prefer Tasso, or even that sleepy tale-teller Ariosto.'

'May I take the liberty to ask, sir, if you do not take great pleasure from reading Horace?'

'There are maxims in this writer from which a man of the world may get some benefit; and the expressive energy of the verse fixes them more easily in the memory. But I care little for his journey to Brindisi, and his account of a bad dinner; or for his fishwives' quarrel between one Rupilius, whose words he describes as being "full of poisonous filth", and some other person, whose words were "dipped in vinegar". I was disgusted by his coarse lampoons against old women and witches; nor do I see the merit of his telling his friend Mæcenas that, if he will but rank him amongst lyric poets, his "lofty head shall touch the stars". Fools have a habit of believing that everything written by a famous author is admirable. For my part, I read only to please myself, and like only what suits my taste.'

Candide, who had been brought up never to form an opinion of his own, was astonished at all this. Martin, how-ever, thought Pococurante's attitude very reasonable.

'Ah, here's a Cicero', said Candide. 'This great man, I fancy, you are never tired of reading!'

'I never read him at all. What do I care for his pleadings for Rabirius or Cluentius? I try causes enough myself. I might have got along better with his philosophic works—except that, when I found he doubted of everything, I concluded that I knew as much as he, and had no need of a guide to ignorance.'

'Ah, but see these four-score volumes of Memoirs of the Academy of Sciences', said Martin. 'There may be some-thing good there.'

'There would be, if any of the compilers of this rubbish

had so much as invented the art of pin-making. But all these books are filled with empty abstractions, without one item of practical use.'

'What a prodigious number of plays!' said Candide, turning to another group of shelves: 'in Italian, in Spanish, in French!'

'Yes, there are three thousand of them, and not three good ones. And as for all these collections of sermons, which all put together are not worth a page of Seneca, and all these volumes of theology—you can well believe that neither I nor anyone else ever opens them.'

Martin noticed some shelves of English books. 'I fancy', he said to the senator, 'that a Republican like yourself must take pleasure in most of these works, imbued as they are with so liberal a spirit.'

'Yes, it is fine to write what one thinks: it is the privilege of a man. Throughout Italy, we write only what we do not think. The modern inhabitants of the land of the Cæsars and of Antoninus dare not have a single idea without permission from a Jacobin monk.

'I should be enamoured of the sense of liberty that inspires the geniuses of England, were it not that all that is good in this fair liberty of theirs is corrupted by petty passions and the spirit of party.'

Candide saw a collection of the works of Milton, and asked the senator if he did not think that author a great man. 'Who?' said Pococurante. 'That barbarian who writes a long commentary, in ten books of stumbling verse, on the first chapter of Genesis? That slovenly imitator of the Greeks, who has made grotesque nonsense of the story of the Creation? On the one hand, we have his Moses representing the Deity as making the world from the Word— yet his Messiah takes a large pair of compasses from the heavenly cupboard, to trace out his intended work!

'How could I have any esteem for a writer who has spoiled Tasso's *Hell and Devil*? Who transforms Lucifer sometimes into a toad, and sometimes into a pygmy? Who makes him repeat the same arguments a hundred times, and turns him into a theological casuist? A writer who borrows from Ariosto's comic invention of firearms, and absurdly turns it into a grave tale of the devils firing off canon in heaven?

'Neither I nor any other Italian can take any pleasure in all these dreary extravagances. The *Marriage of Sin and Death*, and all that account of Sin delivering snakes from her womb, are enough to make a man of any sensibility vomit. As for that long description of a hospital—it is fit reading only for a sexton.

'This obscure, bizarre and disgusting poem was slighted at its first publication. I only treat the author now as he was treated in his own country by his contemporaries.

'Such are my sentiments. I speak my mind, and am perfectly indifferent whether others think as I do.'

Candide was grieved, for he had a great respect for Homer, and was rather fond of Milton. 'Alas,' he whispered to Martin, 'I fear that this man must hold our German poets in great contempt.'

'There would be no great harm in that', said Martin.

'What a superior being!' Candide muttered between his teeth. 'What a great genius is this Pococurante! Nothing is good enough for him.'

They next went down to the garden, and Candide complimented the senator on its various adornments. 'It is all in very bad taste', said the owner. ''Tis a mere collection of gewgaws. But tomorrow I shall have another laid out upon a grander scale.'

When the two sightseers had taken leave of His Excellency, Candide remarked to Martin: 'Well, I think that now you will own that we have met the happiest of mortals—for he feels himself superior to everything that he possesses.'

'Do you not see', said Martin, 'that everything he possesses disgusts him? Plato has observed that the best stomachs are not those that reject all food.'

'But there must be some pleasure in condemning everything—in perceiving faults where others think they see beauties.'

'You mean, there is pleasure in having no pleasure.'

'Well, well, it seems that the only happy man will be I myself, when I see Cunégonde again.'

'It is always good to hope.'

But the days and weeks passed by, with no news of Cacambo. Candide was so overwhelmed with grief that he did not even notice the ingratitude of Paquette and Friar Giroflée, who never came to see him.

CHAPTER XXVI

SUPPER WITH SIX KINGS

CANDIDE, Martin and the other guests at the inn were just going to supper, when a man with a face the colour of soot came up behind Candide, took him by the arm, and said: 'Hold yourself ready to go along with us, without fail.'

It was Cacambo. Almost beside himself with joy, Candide embraced his dear friend. 'Cunégonde must be here too, I suppose?' he said. 'Where is she? Lead me to her, that I may die of joy in her presence!'

'Cunégonde is not here', said Cacambo. 'She is at Constantinople.'

'Good Heavens, Constantinople! But no matter—if she were in China, I would fly thither. Let us be gone!'

'We will go after supper. I can say no more to you now.

I am a slave, and my master waits for me. I must go and attend him at table. But say not a word, only get your supper and hold yourself ready.'

In a turmoil of emotions—delighted to have met his faithful agent again, astonished to hear that he was a slave, obsessed with the prospect of recovering his mistress— Candide sat down to supper. At table with him were Martin, who had listened unemotionally to his conversation with Cacambo, and six strangers who had come to Venice to take part in the carnival.

Cacambo, who was in attendance upon one of these strangers, said to him towards the end of the meal: 'Sire, Your Majesty can go when he pleases, the ship is ready.' After saying this, he left the room. The guests at the other tables looked at each other in surprise, but said nothing.

Another servant went up to his master, and said: 'Sire, Your Majesty's chaise is at Padua, and the bark is ready'. At a sign from the master, the servant withdrew.

The surprise of the company grew. A third servant went up to a third of the strangers, and said: 'Sire, believe me, Your Majesty had better not make any longer stay in this place. I will go and get everything ready.' This servant also immediately went out.

Candide and Martin took it for granted that these people were characters in a carnival masquerade. A fourth servant said to a fourth master: 'Your Majesty may set off when he pleases', and also went out. A fifth servant said the same to a fifth master. A sixth servant, however—whose master was sitting next to Candide—made a different remark. 'Troth, Sire,' he said, 'they will no longer trust Your Majesty, nor myself neither. We may both of us be sent to jail this very night. I go to make my own arrangements—and so, Sire, adieu.'

The six strangers, Candide and Martin sat in deep silence, until Candide broke it. 'Gentlemen,' he said, 'this is very droll. How came you all to be kings? I must confess that my friend Martin here and myself are but commoners.'

Cacambo's master answered gravely, in Italian: 'I am not joking. My name is Achmet III.[1] For many years I was Grand Sultan. I dethroned my brother, my nephew dethroned me; my viziers were beheaded, and I pass my declining years in the Old Seraglio. My nephew, the Grand Sultan Mahomet, gives me permission to travel sometimes for my health; and I am come to spend the carnival at Venice.'

A young man who sat next to Achmet spoke next: 'My name is Ivan.[2] I was once Czar of all the Russias, but was dethroned in my cradle. My father and mother were imprisoned, and I was brought up in jail. I am sometimes allowed to travel, accompanied by my warders; and I am come to spend the carnival at Venice.'

A third said: 'I am Charles Edward,[3] King of England. My father abdicated the throne in my favour. I have fought in defence of my rights, and eight hundred of my friends have had their hearts torn out of their bodies and thrown in their faces. I myself have been confined in a prison. I am going to Rome to visit the King my father, who was dethroned like myself and my grandfather; and I am come to spend the carnival at Venice.'

The fourth said: 'I am the King of Poland.[4] The fortune

[1] Succeeded his brother, Mustapha II, in 1703. Dethroned by the Janissaries in 1730, died in 1736.

[2] Born in 1730, dethroned in the same year, imprisoned, and finally stabbed to death in 1762.

[3] 'Bonnie Prince Charlie', the Young Pretender. He died in Florence in 1788.

[4] Augustus, Elector of Saxony and King of Poland, expelled from his kingdom in the war of 1756.

of war has stripped me of my dominions. My father suffered the same mishap. I resign myself to the will of Providence, like Sultan Achmet, Czar Ivan and King Charles Edward, whom God long preserve; and I am come to spend the carnival at Venice.'

The fifth said: 'I am King of Poland also.[1] I have twice lost my kingdom; but Providence has given me another domain, where I have done more good than all the Sarmatian kings put together were ever able to do on the banks of the Vistula. I resign myself likewise to Providence; and I am come to spend the carnival at Venice.'

The sixth monarch said: 'Gentlemen, I am not so great a prince as any of you. But I am, for all that, a king like any other. I am Theodore, elected King of Corsica.[2] I have had the title of Majesty, and now am scarcely granted the title of "Signor". I have minted my own money, and now do not possess a farthing. I have had two Secretaries of State, and now scarcely have a valet. I once sat on a throne, and since then have lain upon a truss of straw in a London jail. I very much fear that I shall meet the same fate here, although I am but come, like Your Majesties, to spend the carnival at Venice.'

This last utterance filled the other five kings with noble compassion. Each of them gave King Theodore twenty sequins with which to buy some suits of clothes and shirts. Candide gave him a diamond worth two thousand sequins.

---

[1] Stanislas Leszczynski, father-in-law of Louis XV, after losing the throne of Poland received the non-hereditary sovereignty of the Duchies of Bar and Lorraine, where he won the title 'The Beneficent'.

[2] Baron Theodor Neuhof, born in Metz in 1690, soldier of fortune who helped the Corsicans to rebel against the Genoese and was proclaimed their king, but left Corsica in fear of assassination eight months later. Died in London in 1756.

'Who is this man,' said one of the kings, 'who is able to give—and, what is more, has given—a hundred times as much as each of us? Are you also a king, sir?'

'No, sir,' said Candide, 'and I do not wish to be.'

As they were leaving the table, four Serene Highnesses came in. They also had lost their territories, and had come to spend the remainder of the carnival at Venice. But Candide paid no attention to these newcomers: all that he cared about was to go to Constantinople in search of Cunégonde.

CHAPTER XXVII

VOYAGE TO CONSTANTINOPLE

CACAMBO had hired cabins for Candide and Martin on the Turkish ship that was to carry Sultan Achmet back to Constantinople. After prostrating themselves before his unhappy Highness, they embarked.

'How strange to sup with six kings,' said Candide, as they were going on board, 'and one of them so poor that I gave him charity! Perhaps there may be many other princes still more unfortunate.

'For my part, I have lost only eighty sheep laden with treasure, and I am flying to the arms of Cunégonde. I say it once more, my dear Martin: Pangloss was in the right —everything is for the best.'

'I hope it may be.'

'But truly, was not that an improbable adventure? Never before has anyone seen or heard of six dethroned monarchs supping together at an inn.'

'It is not more extraordinary than most of the things that have happened to us. It is not unusual for kings to be dethroned; and as for our having had the honour to sup with six of them, it is a mere trifle, unworthy of note. What does it matter with whom one sups, so long as the fare is good?'

On board the vessel Candide fell on the neck of his old servant and friend Cacambo. 'What news of Cunégonde?' he said. 'Is she still a paragon of beauty? Does she still love me? How does she do? You have doubtless purchased a palace for her at Constantinople.'

'My dear master, Cunégonde washes dishes on the banks of the Propontis, in the house of a prince who has very few dishes to wash. She is a slave of a former sovereign named Rakoczy,[1] to whom the Grand Turk allows three crowns a day to maintain him in his exile. What is worse, she has lost her beauty and is grown very ugly.'

'Ugly or handsome, I am a man of honour, and am bound to love her always. But how can she have been reduced to such an abject condition, with the five or six millions that you brought her?'

'I will tell you. First, I was obliged to give two millions to Señor Don Fernando d'Ibarro y Figueora y Mascarenes y Lampourdos y Souza, Governor of Buenos Aires, for liberty to take Mistress Cunégonde away with me. Then a pirate stripped us of the rest. This same pirate carried us to Cape Matapan, to Milo, to Nicaria, to Samos, to Petra, to the Dardanelles and to Scutari. Cunégonde and the old woman are now in the house of the prince I told you of, and I myself am slave to the dethroned Sultan.'

'What a chain of dreadful disasters! But, after all, I still have some diamonds left. I can easily set Cunégonde free. . . It is a pity that she is grown ugly.

[1] Ferencz Rakoczy, a Transylvanian prince, stirred the Hungarians to revolt against the Hapsburgs, and fought successively against Leopold I and Joseph I. Finally defeated, he retired to Turkey and died at Rodosto in 1735.

'What think you?' Candide continued, speaking now to Martin. 'Who is most to be pitied, Sultan Achmet, Czar Ivan, King Charles Edward or I?'

'I cannot tell. To find the answer, I would have to enter into all your hearts.'

'Ah, if Pangloss were here, he would know the answer, and would tell us it.'

'I know not in what balance your Pangloss can weigh human misfortunes. I suppose, however, that there are millions of men on earth who are a hundred times more to be pitied than King Charles Edward, Czar Ivan or Sultan Achmet.'

'That may well be.'

A few days later they reached the entrance to the Black Sea. Candide paid a heavy ransom for Cacambo, and they and Martin transferred themselves to a galley that would take them to the shore of the Propontis. However ugly Cunégonde might have become, Candide was resolved to find her.

Amongst the crew of convicts on this galley were two who rowed very awkwardly, so that the Levantine captain kept lashing their bare backs with a bull's pizzle. Candide noticed them especially, as he felt sorry for them. Their disfigured features seemed rather like those of Pangloss and the unlucky Jesuit baron, Cunégonde's brother. The resemblance touched and saddened Candide, and he looked at the two men still more attentively. 'In troth,' he said to Cacambo, 'if I had not seen Master Pangloss hanged, and myself had the misfortune to kill the Baron, I should believe that they were among the rowers.'

On hearing the words 'Pangloss' and 'the Baron', the two convicts uttered a cry and stopped rowing, letting go of the oars. The Levantine captain rushed up to them and applied his bull's pizzle harder than ever. 'Hold, hold, signor,' Candide shouted, 'I will give you all the money you ask!'

'Why, it is Candide!' the two convicts exclaimed.

'Do I dream?' said Candide. 'Am I awake? Am I actually on board this galley? Is this my Lord Baron, whom I killed? And Master Pangloss, whom I saw hanged?'

'Yes, 'tis we, 'tis we!'

'What, is this the great philosopher?' said Martin.

'Hark ye, captain,' said Candide, 'what ransom do you ask for the Baron von Thunder-ten-Tronckh, one of the first barons of the Reich, and for Dr. Pangloss, the most profound metaphysician in Germany?'

'Dog of a Christian,' said the Levantine, 'since these two dogs of Christian convicts are barons and metaphysicians—which doubtless are high titles in their country—why, then, thou shalt give me fifty thousand sequins.'

'You shall have them, sir. Carry me back with the speed of lightning to Constantinople, and you shall be paid immediately. No! Rather carry me first to Mistress Cunégonde.'

But the captain had already, on hearing the first order, started turning the ship round on a course for Constantinople. He made the crew row so hard that the vessel seemed to fly like a bird.

Candide embraced the Baron and Pangloss again and again. 'And how is it, my dear Baron, that I did not kill you? And you, my dear Pangloss, how are you come to life again after your hanging? And why are you both on this Turkish galley?'

'Is it true that my dear sister is in this country?' 'Is it really my dear Candide?' asked the Baron and Pangloss.

'Yes, it is', said Candide to both questions. He introduced Martin and Cacambo to the two others, and there were embraces and voluble conversation all round.

The galley quickly brought them to port, and a Jewish merchant was fetched, to whom Candide sold for fifty thousand sequins a diamond worth double that amount— although the Jew swore by Abraham that he could not give more. Pangloss and the Baron were set free: the former flung himself weeping at the feet of his benefactor, whilst the latter nodded his thanks, and promised to return the money at the first opportunity.

'But is it possible', the Baron asked, 'that my sister should be in Turkey?'

'It is more than possible; it is certain', said Candide. 'She scours the dishes in the house of a Transylvanian prince.'

Two more Jews were fetched, Candide sold more diamonds, and they all set out, in another galley, to liberate Cunégonde.

CHAPTER XXVIII

THE GALLEY-SLAVES' STORIES

'ONCE again, I ask your pardon, Reverend Father,' said Candide, 'for running you through the body.'

'Let us say no more about it. I must own that I myself was a little hasty. But since you wish to know by what accident I came to be on board that galley, I will tell you.

'The College apothecary cured me of the wound you gave me. Some time afterwards I was attacked and taken prisoner by a party of Spanish troops, who clapped me in prison at Buenos Aires, just after my sister had left that city.

'I asked leave to return to Rome, to see the General of my order. He appointed me chaplain to the French ambassador at Constantinople.

'I had not been a week in my new office, when I met one evening a very handsome young *icoglan*. The weather was hot, and the young man had an inclination to bathe. I took the opportunity to bathe likewise. I did not know that it was a capital crime for a Christian to be found naked with a young Mussulman. A cadi ordered me to receive a hundred blows on the soles of my feet, and sent me to the galleys—a most horrible injustice!

'But now I would fain know, how came my sister to be here in Turkey as scullion to a Transylvanian prince?'

'But you, my dear Pangloss,' said Candide, 'how comes it that I see you again?'

'You saw me hanged, as you thought', said Pangloss. 'I ought properly to have been burnt; but, as you will remember, it rained in torrents just as they were about to roast me. They could not even light the fire: so they hanged me, because they could do no better.

'A surgeon bought my body, carried me home and dissected me. He began by making a crucial incision from my navel to the clavicle.

'I had been shockingly badly hanged. The High Executioner of the Holy Inquisition, who was a subdeacon, was an excellent hand at burning people; but as for hanging, he was not used to it. The cord was wet and did not slip properly, and the noose was not tight. In short, I continued to breathe. The crucial incision made me roar out so loud that the surgeon fell over backwards. He imagined that he had been dissecting the devil, ran away in terror and tumbled down the staircase. The noise brought his wife from an adjoining room. She saw me stretched upon the table with my crucial incision, became still more terrified than her husband, and ran away and fell over him.

'After all this confusion, I heard the wife say to her husband: "My love, how could you think of dissecting a heretic? Don't you know that they have the devil in their bodies? I'll run directly for a priest to come and exorcise him."

'I was horrified at this proposal, and gathered what little strength I had left to cry out: "Mercy! Mercy!" At length the Portuguese barber took courage, and sewed up my wound. His wife nursed me, and in a fortnight I was upon my legs.

'The barber got me a place as lacquey to a Knight of Malta, who was going to Venice. But this man had no money to pay my wages, so I entered the service of a Venetian merchant, and went with him to Constantinople.

'One day I took a notion to enter a mosque. Nobody was there but an old imam and a very pretty young female, who was saying her prayers. Her throat was bare, and in her bosom she had a beautiful nosegay of tulips, roses, anemones, ranunculuses, hyacinths and auriculas. She let her nosegay fall: I picked it up, and most respectfully returned it to her. But I was so long in putting it in place, that the imam grew angry. Seeing that I was a Christian, he cried out for help. They carried me before a cadi, who ordered me to receive a hundred blows on the soles of my feet, and sent me to the galleys.

'I was chained in the very same galley, and to the very same bench, as his lordship. The rest of the crew consisted of four young men from Marseilles, five Neapolitan priests, and two monks from Corfu. I learnt from my fellow-slaves that adventures similar to mine were very common.

'His lordship always claimed that he had suffered a worse injustice than I; but I used to insist that it was much more permissible to replace a nosegay in a young woman's bosom than to be found naked with a young *icoglan*. We were continually disputing this point, and in consequence were frequently lashed with a bull's pizzle. But at last the concatenation of sublunary events brought you on board our galley to ransom us.'

'Tell me, my dear Pangloss, when you had been hanged,

dissected, and whipped, and were tugging at an oar in a galley, did you continue to think that everything was for the best?'

'I retain my first opinion. After all, I am a philosopher, and it would not become me to contradict myself. Besides, Leibnitz cannot be wrong, and the doctrine of the pre-established harmony is the finest thing in the world—as also are the *plenum* and the *materia subtilis*.'

CHAPTER XXIX

CUNÉGONDE FOUND AGAIN

As the party approached the house of the Transylvanian prince, they saw Cunégonde and the old woman hanging cloths on a line.

The Baron turned pale at the sight, and even Candide, that faithful lover, was horrified. The lovely Cunégonde was burnt black by the sun, her eyes were bloodshot, her neck withered, her cheeks wrinkled and her arms covered with a red scurf. Candide recoiled for an instant, but good manners made him go forward. Cunégonde and the old woman embraced Candide and the Baron. Candide then ransomed the two women.

There was a small farm in the neighbourhood, and the old woman suggested that Candide should rent this as a temporary lodging for the whole party. Cunégonde did not know that she had grown ugly, as nobody had told her. She reminded Candide of his promises in so peremptory a manner that the good-natured youth did not dare to refuse her. He told the Baron that he was going to marry his sister.

'I will never suffer such baseness on my sister's part,' said the Baron, 'or such insolence on yours. I will never be reproached with such a disgrace. Why, my sister's children would not be received in the chapter-houses of Germany! No, my sister shall never marry any person below the rank of a baron of the Reich.'

Cunégonde fell weeping at her brother's feet, but he was inflexible. 'Silly fellow,' said Candide, 'have I not delivered thee from the galleys, paid thy ransom and thy sister's, too, who was a dish-washer and is very ugly? I have the goodness to make her my wife, and thou still dost set thyself up to oppose the match! If I were to give rein to my anger, I should kill thee again.'

'Thou mayst kill me again,' said the Baron, 'but thou shalt not marry my sister while I am living.'

CHAPTER XXX

PHILOSOPHY ON THE PROPONTIS

AT the bottom of his heart Candide had no wish to marry Cunégonde. But the Baron's insolence made him determined to do so, and Cunégonde pressed him so warmly that he could not recant.

He consulted Pangloss, Martin and Cacambo. Pangloss drew up a fine memorial proving that the Baron had no rights over his sister, and that by the laws of the Reich she could marry Candide morganatically. Martin advised throwing the Baron into the sea. Cacambo suggested that he should be handed over to the Levantine skipper and put back to work in the galleys: after which he could be sent by the first ship to the Father General in Rome.

This suggestion found general favour. The old woman was told of it, and approved, but nothing was said about it to Cunégonde. The transaction was carried out, for a little money: and they had the double pleasure of tricking a Jesuit and punishing the pride of a German baron.

The reader might well suppose that Candide—having, after so many misadventures, got married to his mistress; being blessed with the company of the philosophers Pangloss and Martin, the shrewd Cacambo and the old woman; and having, moreover, brought back so many diamonds from the land of the ancient Incas—would now live happily ever afterwards.

What in fact happened was this: Candide was so badly cheated by the Jews that in the end he had nothing but his little farm. His wife, who grew uglier every day, became sour-tempered and insupportable. The old woman was ailing, and became even worse-humoured than Cunégonde. Cacambo, who worked in the garden and carried its produce to market in Constantinople, became worn out with toil and felt utterly miserable. Pangloss was gloomy at not being a shining light in some German university. As for Martin, he was convinced that one is equally badly off wherever one is, so he bore everything with patience.

Candide, Martin and Pangloss sometimes had discussions on metaphysics and ethics. Boats passed under the windows of the farm, carrying effendis, pashas and cadis off to exile in Lemnos, Mitylene or Erzerum. Other cadis, pashas and effendis could be seen coming to replace the exiles, and later being exiled in their turn. The boats also carried heads, neatly fixed on poles, which were being sent as gifts to the Sublime Porte. Such sights increased the philosophers' zeal for argument.

When they were not arguing, time hung so heavily on their hands that one day the old woman remarked: 'I wonder which is worse: to be ravished a hundred times by negro pirates, to have one buttock cut off, to run the gauntlet among the Bulgarians, to be dissected and to be a galley-slave; or to stay here doing nothing?'

'That', said Candide, 'is a very profound question.' It started them off on further discussions. Martin had come to the conclusion that it is man's fate to live either in agonies of fear and turmoil or in the prostration of boredom. Candide did not entirely agree, but could not make up his mind. Pangloss, whilst admitting that he had undergone dreadful sufferings, still maintained that everything was marvellously good—although he did not believe it.

Something happened that confirmed Martin in his detestable beliefs, made Candide hesitate more than ever, and even caused embarrassment to Pangloss. This was the arrival of Paquette and Friar Giroflée. They were penniless, having quickly run through the three thousand piastres that Candide had given them. They had parted, been reconciled and had quarrelled again. They had been imprisoned, and had escaped. Friar Giroflée had turned Turk as he once said he might. Paquette continued to ply her trade wherever she went, but earned little by it.

'I told you', Martin said to Candide, 'that your gift would soon be squandered, and would only make them more miserable. You and Cacambo have poured out millions of piastres, yet you are no happier than Friar Giroflée and Paquette.'

Pangloss had a few observations to make to Paquette. 'So, my poor child,' he said, 'Heaven has brought you here among us again. Do you know that you have cost me the tip of my nose, one eye and one ear? Ah me, to what have you been reduced—and what a world is this of ours!'

This new event made them all philosophize more than ever.

There lived in the neighbourhood a very famous dervish, who was generally considered the best philosopher in Turkey. One day they went to consult him. Pangloss, as their spokesman, said to the dervish: 'Master, we come to entreat you to tell us, why so strange an animal as man was created?'

'Why do you meddle with the matter?' said the dervish. 'Is it any business of yours?'

'But, Reverend Father,' said Candide, 'there is a horrible deal of evil on earth.'

'What signifies it whether there is evil or good? When the Sultan sends a ship to Egypt, does he trouble his head whether the rats in the hold are at ease or not?'

'What, then, should one do?'

'One should be silent.'

'I offered myself the flattering prospect', said Candide, 'of debating with you a little concerning causes and effects, the best of possible worlds, the origin of evil, the nature of the soul, the pre-established harmony, and similar matters.'

At these words the dervish shut the door in their faces.

That same day news had come from Constantinople that two Viziers of the Bench and the Grand Mufti had been strangled, and that several of their friends had been impaled. This catastrophe caused a considerable stir for a few hours. On their way back from the dervish's house, the philosophers met a worthy old man taking the air at his door, under an arbour of orange-trees. Pangloss, who besides being a philosopher was also keenly interested in gossip, asked him if he knew the name of the strangled Mufti.

'No,' said the old man, 'I have never in my life known the name of any Mufti or Vizier; nor do I know anything of the event you speak of. I take the view that, in general, those who meddle in politics tend to come to miserable ends, and deserve to do so. But I never inquire what is doing at Constantinople. I am contented with sending thither for sale the fruits of my garden.'

He invited the foreigners into his house, where his two daughters and two sons brought them home-made sherbets of various kinds, of caymac flavoured with the peels of candied citrons, oranges, lemons, pineapples, dates, pistachio nuts and Mocha coffee—which last was unadulterated with the inferior coffee of Batavia or the American islands. After this the two daughters perfumed the guests' beards.

'You must have a very large estate', Candide said to the old man.

'I have no more than twenty acres, which I dig with the help of my children. Labour holds off three great evils: tedium, vice and poverty.'

On their way home, Candide thought over the old Turk's words. 'This old worthy', said he, 'seems to have created for himself a destiny highly preferable to those of the six kings with whom we supped.'

'Elevated stations', said Pangloss, 'are often very dangerous: so all the philosophers testify. Eglon, King of Moab, was assassinated by Aod. Absalom was hanged by his hair and run through with three darts. King Nadab, son of Jeroboam, was killed by Baaza; King Ela by Zimri; Okosias by Jehu; Athaliah by Jehoiada. The Kings Jehoiakim, Jeconiah and Zedekiah were led into captivity. You know what befel Crœsus, Astyages, Darius, Dionysus of Syracuse, Pyrrhus, Perseus, Hannibal, Jugurtha, Ariovistus, Cæsar, Pompey, Nero, Otho, Vitellius, Domitian, Richard II of England, Edward II, Henry VI, Richard III, Mary Stuart, Charles I, the three Henries of France and the Emperor Henry IV. You know also—'

'I know also', said Candide, 'that we must dig in our garden.'

'You are in the right,' said Pangloss, 'for when man was put into the garden of Eden he was put there *ut operaretur eum*—that he might till it, that he might work: which proves that man was not born to be idle.'

'Let us work, then, and not argue', said Martin. 'It is the only way to render life supportable.'

All the members of the little society entered into this laudable design, and set themselves to exercise their various talents. Their small farm yielded good crops. Cunégonde continued to be very ugly, but she became an excellent pastrycook. Paquette embroidered. The old woman laundered. Even Friar Giroflée turned out useful: he proved to be a very good carpenter, and even quite a decent fellow.

Pangloss would often say to Candide: 'There is certainly a concatenation of events in this best of all possible worlds. Consider: had you not been kicked out of a fine castle for love of Mistress Cunégonde—had you not come under the Inquisition—had you not travelled over America on foot—had you not run the Baron through the body—had you not lost your sheep from the good country of El Dorado—why, then, you would not now be here, to eat candied citrons and pistachio nuts.'

'That is excellently observed', said Candide. 'But let us dig in our garden.'